# SIMULATION

## THE DAWN OF A SUPERHERO

*"When passion runs too hot!"*

SAM SKYBORNE

DUKEBOX.LIFE

Published by DukeBox.life.
http://DukeBox.life.

*To all my girls and fellow sci-fi female superhero fans, with love!*

"Logic will get you from A to B.
Imagination will take you everywhere."

Albert Einstein

# PROLOGUE

Samantha Fielding woke to a throbbing ache in her shoulders. She was slumped forward, her arms tied too tightly behind her, to the back of a rusted metal chair. She tried to move. Every part of her screamed in agony. Her short, blond hair stuck to her face where blood and sweat had glued it in place. She could taste sand and blood in her mouth, and her throat was dry, making it impossible to swallow.

Around her, the scorching sun cleaved through the numerous bullet holes in the wooden walls and sliced through the thick, dark, dusty air inside the sweltering shed. On the floor at her feet lay the lifeless bodies of her Unit—her friends—her family. She felt thick, rancid bile rise in her throat as she retched at the memories.

She had no idea how long she had been unconscious. She had lost all sense of time from the moment they were ambushed and captured.

The War had been raging for so long that no one really knew what they were fighting for any more. Smaller, weaker nations and cultures had been assimilated into greater powers, or simply wiped from the face of the earth. Those that were strong enough to survive were turned into finely tuned killing machines. Soldiers' lives were cheap, and once captured, pretty much worthless. The up side of this was that any troops who got caught were at least assured of a swift death.

Unfortunately, Sam and her Unit had not been that lucky. They were kept alive, if only barely, and repeatedly beaten and tortured in what seemed like an endless cycle. What made it even worse for Sam was that she had been singled out, kept tied to a chair and made to watch the agony being inflicted on people she cared about and loved. Each lash, each injury, each torturous moment she observed, was burnt into her retinae and tore at her heart, but Sam forced herself to watch and remember every detail so, in the unlikely event she survived, she could do her job and tell the world how brave each and every one of them had been.

The familiar sound of marching army boots on the dusty dirt tracks brought her focus back to her immediate surroundings. She prayed quietly that this time it would finally mean the end of the waiting, the end of her misery.

The door flew open and two foot-soldiers marched in ahead of their Captain. He was a looming, grotesque, bearded man, who chewed incessantly at the tip of a cigar.

"Oh goody. My turn," Sam said hoarsely, her throat grinding out each word through the pain, "I was beginning to feel left out."

Behind the Captain, a statuesque, raven-haired female stood quietly, the perfect combination of lethal physical power and devastating grace. Sam recognised her as their Sergeant.

"So what will it be today? Just you and me?" Sam taunted the Captain, and then looked the Sergeant up and down. "Or do you fancy a little threesome?"

Sam noticed, with satisfaction, that the Captain's lip curled in annoyance behind the cigar, revealing brown stained teeth. He nodded at the Sergeant who then stepped forward.

"Ah, you're in the mood for a little girl on girl act—"

The first blow was a sharp right hook to the side of Sam's face that knocked her sideways, splitting her lip. She drew on all her strength and slowly righted herself as much as her restraints would allow. "That's right Honey." She spat out the blood. "Don't hold back, 'cause you know I like it a little rough."

A shower of body blows and punches to the face followed in quick succession, but Sam locked her gaze onto the crystal blue eyes of her assailant, refusing to cower.

The assault stopped.

The salty copper taste filled Sam's mouth as a new wave of fresh blood pooled and then dripped from her mouth, landing with an unnaturally loud thud onto the sandy floor in front of her.

"She's only the reporter." The Sergeant's voice was barely audible over the roar in Sam's ears. "Is this really necessary, Sir?"

The Captain slowly removed the thick soggy cigar from his fleshy lips and, in a cool patronising tone explained, "That is precisely why it is necessary. People like her make or break a nation. One thought, one idea, can change destiny."

A few seconds later Sam felt the sharp pain in her neck and shoulders as the Sergeant wrenched her head back by her hair.

"Oh good. I was worried you'd had enough," Sam said, trying to smile.

The Sergeant once again laid into her, with increased vigour. However, this time Sam did not miss the distant look in her assailant's eyes. She realised that in that moment the Sergeant was blind to her, waging a battle against demons within that had very little to do with her. She wondered what nightmares could be fuelling such hatred and aggression.

Once the next wave of blows subsided, Sam became aware of movement in her peripheral vision.

"Make sure they're all dead before you torch the place," the Captain called back over his shoulder as he headed out the door, taking one of the foot soldiers with him.

It only took a couple more well aimed blows before Sam toppled forward to the ground.

The Sergeant stayed bent over, resting her hands on her knees, until she had caught her breath. She stood up, wiped the sweat from her brow and headed toward the door.

The remaining soldier took that as his cue and stepped forward to finish the job with a bullet to Sam's head, but before he could pull the trigger, the Sergeant stopped him with a hand to the shoulder.

"Enough!" Her eyes flashed a warning.

The soldier hesitated only briefly before backing down and following her out.

Sam tried to open her eyes. They were thick and swollen but she could just about make out her surroundings. Bright flames were all around her, eating up the wooden walls with thick billows of smoke, making it even harder to see. She was lying half on her side, still bound to the chair. She tried to move. All she needed to do was somehow crawl a few feet to the door—to freedom. But the tight restraints and the angular metal corners of the chair dug deep into her arms and back, forcing her body into an unnatural contorted position. The smooth sandy floor made it hard to gain traction. It quickly became clear that she was not going to make it.

Her body and senses were wired from the adrenaline coursing through her veins. She was aware of the irony of never feeling more alive than in that moment, whilst fighting for her life. She could feel every splinter, lump and bump in the floor beneath her, the searing heat of the metal chair burning into her skin, the flames licking at her feet. She longed to succumb to the sweet, soothing void of unconsciousness. This was the punishment she deserved for letting her Unit die, for letting Sabrina die. Defeated, she rested her head on the floor and waited for her agonising death to come.

Just then, large, dusty boots appeared inches from her face. The acrid smoke seared her eyes. All she could see was a formless face, as soft cool hands gripped her shoulders and dragged her to safety before she finally lost consciousness.

# 1

Sam gasped awake. Her heart pounded in her chest. A sheen of cold sweat covered her half naked body, making her white vest and dog-tags stick to her skin.

She sat up, her eyes frantically searching her surroundings. Relief and helpless regret flooded her body as she realised she was safe in her bed in the small coastal cottage, overlooking St Ives Bay, in Cornwall. The harrowing memories of her Unit being captured and tortured regularly plagued her dreams. She rubbed her eyes in an attempt to wipe the images of her friends being raped, tortured and murdered from her mind. The pain, the searing guilt and the feeling of complete helplessness enveloped her. She often wished that she had not been rescued from those flames. Her Angel of Mercy was really a Demon of Torment, trapping her in a particular sadistic sort of hell. She was the sole survivor and thus the only one left to bear witness. She felt trapped between the desperate need to forget and the duty of honouring the memory of her beloved dead.

An unopened olive army duffle-bag and worn, partly

scorched boots lying on the floor were the only signs that life had returned to the otherwise pale, abandoned bedroom where white dust sheets still covered most of the humble furniture.

She got up and went over to a small white washstand with an oval mirror. She poured some water from the porcelain jug into the basin and rinsed her face, enjoying the feeling of the cool liquid on her feverish skin. She dried off and examined herself in the mirror. She seemed thinner than she remembered, her face more angular. Old, blue grey eyes stared back at her. She tried to remember what she used to look like before The War.

The War had changed so much, but most of all it had changed the human spirit. It had taught her the most valuable lesson of her life: any semblance of control was an illusion. In fact it was a delusion. She had no more power to affect her destiny or the fate of anyone around her than someone tossed far out in the deep stormy ocean, caught in the tumultuous currents that pulled them ever deeper. All a person could do was fight, tread water, and hope to stay alive long enough for someone to find them, or surrender and drown.

She noticed the chain hanging from one of the mirror supports. She ran her fingers along the cool metal links until she gently held a small silver lighthouse pendant in her palm. It was a miniature replica of the Godrevy lighthouse that was visible outside through the window. The lighthouse, the pendant and the cottage were bequests from her grandmother. They, like The Lighthouse Pub a couple of miles down the coast, had been in her family for generations.

It was early February and the stormy, grey sea and hostile elements battered the lighthouse and the coastline alike. Sam wrapped her jacket tighter around her as she strode to The Lighthouse Pub.

The countryside around her looked bare. What used to be a thriving English coastal village had now been reduced to barely a skeleton of its former self. There were no crops sown, fences and buildings were broken, and even the old stone walls breached by the storms were unrepaired. Sheds and barns had collapsed and there was no sign of the livestock that once used to roam the hills. The evident poverty and hardship were the consequences of a country engaged in over a decade of war. All the available resources, including both men and women of fighting age, had been shipped off to defend the civilised world. Very few people ever returned.

She was regarded as one of the 'lucky' ones who made it home. Came back to what, she thought, a country of helpless people struggling to survive while they prayed that a war beyond their control would end?

Quite early in the war effort, once they had glimpsed the potential downward spiral such a war would have on society, most people eagerly relinquished their freedoms in favour of the promise of stability, strength and order offered by a strong military state. At first this loss of freedom seemed to be a small price to pay as the war rapidly brought the entire country to its knees and all feared both the enemy and spies within. The rule of law became a lifeline, creating an illusion of control in a world that was crumbling.

However, structure and order to protect the

population soon evolved into something more sinister. The iron fist of the State soon promoted and then harshly enforced an extreme, conservative charter which removed a long list of freedoms and previously protected civil liberties. This charter proclaimed the single New State religion to be New Catholic. Anybody practicing any other religion, or expressing any political view opposed to the construction of a "Better State", or caught engaging in any of the other proclaimed unlawful activities, like homosexuality, were charged under the new Zero Tolerance Policy and taken to endure a fate far worse than death.

In a time when the population was severely diminished, putting your own people to death or keeping criminals imprisoned was regarded as a waste of precious resources. Instead, a new technology had been developed that enabled human beings to be Reset and recycled—like electronics, reset to factory defaults and then reprogrammed to become new, beneficial contributors to society.

---

Inside The Lighthouse Pub it was warm and cosy, a welcoming refuge. Although it was still quite early the pub was alive with the buzz of locals enjoying their first ale of the day.

Behind the bar counter Megs, an older, softer, more curvy version of Sam, held two fingers to her forehead and was pretending to try to mind read one of the customers, a Mr Bow. He was a slight, well weathered man of indeterminate age, somewhere between forty and sixty, who could easily have been mistaken for a low life vagabond if it weren't for his slightly posh accent.

"Have you got it yet?" Mr Bow asked, unconsciously pushing around an empty pint glass.

"No. Sorry. Not yet." Megs shook her head. "Have you had your breakfast yet?"

Sam caught Meg's eye as she quietly slipped onto a barstool at the end of the bar.

Megs beamed her a warm, welcoming smile. "I was beginning to think you'd left again." Megs bent down to move a heavy barrel on the floor.

"Here, let me help with that," Sam offered and ducked under the hatch in the bar counter. Between the two of them they rolled the barrel closer to the door to the back room.

"You know we could really do with all the help we can get around here." Megs said only slightly out of breath. "I think you'd make a great Publican."

"What? And drink up all your profits?" Sam laughed. "No, Grams was right to leave this in your capable hands." Sam glanced around the pub. "Besides you don't need my help. Looks like you are thriving. This is a real refuge for this community. They love you." Sam smiled at her sister. Sam always admired how incredibly positive and strong Megs was, but for the first time she noticed that The War had taken its toll, even on her. She seemed smaller, older and more vulnerable than Sam remembered.

Just then, Pete, a lean, ruggedly handsome, Atlas of a man appeared from the back carrying a new full barrel of ale.

"You remember Pete?" Megs asked, affectionately rubbing Pete's arm as he came to stand next to her. "Pete, you remember my sister, Sam?"

Sam recognised Pete instantly. At school he was a couple of years ahead of her, in the same year as Megs, and he had asked her out a couple of times.

Pete expertly lowered the barrel to safety and smiled broadly as he took Sam's hand in both of his and shook it warmly. "How could one forget? Welcome back."

Sam was surprised by Pete's warm greeting. He was a handsome man, and although he was not her type, she had to admit that it felt really good to be appreciated by another living, breathing human being. It had been a long time since anyone had looked at her like that.

"See, I'm not the only one who'd be glad to have you around." Megs said as she slapped Pete gently on the shoulder with her dishcloth. Pete took the hint and let go of Sam's hand.

"Maybe we can catch up later?" Pete asked.

Sam nodded.

Pete smiled at her one last time before he turned his attention to clearing away the empty barrel they had rolled to the side.

"Oh come on Meggy," Mr Bow interrupted. "Please, try again. I'll crank up the signals this time." He began to fiddle with his ear.

Sam raised an eyebrow and threw Megs a questioning glance.

"PTSD," Megs whispered. "He claims aliens made him a telepath."

"There, try now. A pretty girl like you should be able to read me easily." Mr Bow's lopsided grin revealed a surprisingly perfect set of teeth. Sam wondered what he had been in his previous life, before The War, before whatever tragic events made him into what he was now.

"Oh, but I do," Megs said. She again held up two fingers to her temples and scrunched her eyes closed whilst humming softly. "Nope, still nothing. And no, not even your sweet talking is going to get you another pint before the sun's over the yard arm."

"See, I knew you could do it!" Mr Bow's face lit up. "I have money."

"This is no way to spend your benefit," Megs replied.

"That's what it's for... my benefit," he said, pushing out his chin a little further.

Just then, a short gentleman with a potbelly and a glass eye plonked his empty glass on the counter indicating he was ready for a refill.

"Can I get you something?" Megs asked Sam, heading over to serve the customer.

Sam nodded and then ducked back out from behind the bar to wait for her drink.

Without a moment's hesitation Mr Bow moved his seat closer to her, obviously regarding her as a co-conspirator and, Sam feared, as his new best friend.

"This is England," he mock whispered. "There is hardly ever any sun anyway. How could she know when it's over the yard arm?"

Not wanting to be dragged into an obviously long-standing clash of wills between Megs and Mr Bow, Sam politely excused herself and headed over to peruse the community noticeboard on a nearby wall.

Before The War, people were consumers, devouring products voraciously, then discarding the half-finished, half-used items and moving on to the next, newest, best thing. The War changed all that. All around, in the pub, the town and in people's houses, one could see previously categorised rubbish, materials and discarded items that had been salvaged, resurrected and reused, sometimes in quite ingenious ways. The noticeboard was such an example. It was made from old beermats that had been glued together to form an old fashioned five by seven foot pin-up board. One side served as some sort of remembrance wall, Sam surmised, as she glanced over the neatly pinned faded photographs of young men and women, most of which were annotated with "R.I.P." and names scribbled in faded ink. The other half of the board was overlaid with multiple layers of rough handwritten notes and bits of newspaper cut-outs. Most of the notes were offering services, from waitressing to dog walking and plumbing. A few requested services but were clearly marked "N.L.P"—No to Low Pay.

She needed to find a job. The Forces had given her a reasonable severance and compensation package, which would probably sustain her for another few months, but she knew she needed to think ahead. Besides, she could no longer bear the long, idle hours spent reliving her nightmares. So far, her only respite vacillated between drinking away the pain and taking herself for long coastal runs where she pushed herself to her physical limits, until her muscles and her lungs ached harder than her heart.

Then she saw it. Partially hidden behind a scrawled call for stable hands was a faded but neatly typed note:

SCIENTIFIC RESEARCH TRIALS:
SUBJECTS NEEDED. £50/day.
CONTACT: Nance@PhyCorp.org
TEL: 01209 1954 1956

Sam ripped the note from the board and returned to the bar where Megs had just poured her a golden pint. She noticed Mr Bow lick his lips as he watched Meg place the glass on the table near where Sam had been waiting.

"Know anything about this?" Sam handed Megs the note.

Megs studied it and handed it back shaking her head. "No, but that's a pretty good wage these days."

Mr Bow peered over at the note in Sam's hand. She showed it to him.

Almost instantly his demeanour changed. He recoiled as if physically struck and became very distressed. "No. No. No! You don't w-w-want, want to!"

"It's okay, Mr Bow. Calm, calm... Here." Megs poured and handed him a pint. "You can have your elixir now."

He grabbed the glass with both hands and gulped at it eagerly as if to dowse a fire in his chest.

"That's where the Aliens got me," he finally said once he had gulped down almost half of the pint.

Sam nodded and waited, hoping Mr Bow would enlighten her a bit more, but also not wanting to distress him any further. However, when it became clear that he was not going to discuss the matter any further, she dropped some money on the counter to pay for the pint and headed over to claim a window seat overlooking the bay and the lighthouse in the distance.

---

Two hours later, during her break, Megs brought a cup of coffee over to have with Sam. As she approached she noticed the wistful expression on her little sister's face. Megs followed her eye line. At the next table she recognised the newlyweds for whom she had hosted a little wedding reception the week before. They were laughing and talking intimately as if nothing else existed around them, in that way that only new lovers can. Guessing what was on Sam's mind, Megs' heart went out to her sister.

"So? What adventure are you planning next?" Megs asked trying to add lightness to her tone.

"I'm not sure, yet." Sam refocussed her attention on the glass in front of her, rotating it slowly as she spoke. "I need to find a job."

"Can you keep writing?" Megs asked.

"No, I think I burnt my fingers with that one." Sam shook her head. "Besides, no-one is interested in reading anything which is not related to The War, or getting laid."

"You always were very principled about your art," Megs teased and was pleased to hear the slight laugh that it elicited from her sister.

Megs took a sip of her coffee while taking in the multitude of emotions that flashed across Sam's face as she considered her prospects. "Seriously. What about fiction? You used to be great at writing stories."

Sam looked out of the window.

"Remember how you and Grams used to sit in the conservatory for hours and make up stories. You got your gift from her," Megs said.

"My stories would mostly be illegal now." Sam shook her head.

"Surely you can still write stories, for money, that aren't illegal?"

"Yeah, I could. But I would hate them," Sam laughed. "I'd rather clean toilets." Sam took a sip of her pint.

Megs smiled, remembering the holiday when she and her sister worked at the boys' summer camp doing just that. A long comfortable silence fell between the two sisters as they sat with their own thoughts.

"Will you stay this time?" Megs drained her coffee and set the cup down in the saucer without looking at Sam.

Sam stared into her drink for a long while. "If I can't find another means of escape, then yeah."

"See, we're back to writing porn again," Megs teased as she got up to return to the bar.

## 2

It was early evening. After his shift had finished at 18:00 hours, Pete sauntered over with a pint and came to join Sam. This was followed by an hour or two of animated reminiscing and catching up on the past twenty years since they had been at school together. Finally, when their conversation started drying up, Sam suggested they play a game or two of pool.

Sam had always been a quick study. Even at school, to the frustration of everyone in the class, she seemed to be good at everything she turned her hand to. Her skills at pool were no different. By 21:30 hours they were on their tenth game. Luckily Pete did not seem to mind that he had lost the last seven straight. He seemed entirely preoccupied with flirting with Sam.

Pete was a good looking guy with a boyish charm that Sam suspected gave him yards of leeway with the ladies. What started off as initially quite shy glances and teasing became more audacious as the alcohol flowed. At first Sam felt a little awkward, especially since she did not really know

Pete or anyone in the bar, other than her sister, very well and she tried to discourage his advances firmly but respectfully. However, Pete seemed undeterred, to say the least, and by the end of the tenth round of pool it was getting a little out of hand. Sam had to admit that she did feel quite flattered by his attention and it made her remember how nice it was to be lavished with that kind of affection—affection she had not experienced in a very long time.

Pete had gotten into the way of coming to stand really close behind her as she leaned over the table to aim her cue, forcing her to stand back up into him once she had taken her shot. On this occasion Sam potted three balls in a row to win the game.

Cheers abounded from the happy onlookers.

Sam needed a breather. "I'll go get this round. I feel I've taken advantage by winning all the time."

"I don't mind you taking advantage," Pete replied pulling her into him a little more.

Should have seen that one coming, she thought, before she squirmed out from under him and headed to the bar.

"Two tequilas, please," she asked Megs. It occurred to her that Megs must be working a double shift. "Why are you still behind the bar?"

Megs shrugged. "Oh, I like it. Anyway, if I don't do it we won't be able to stay open."

Sam glanced back to see Pete bantering with a few of his mates before moving over to a smaller table near the window.

"Don't mind him," Megs said nodding in Pete's direction. "He's a bit overly friendly sometimes. He doesn't mean anything by it."

Sam nodded turning back to watch Megs pour the drinks.

"They say home is where the heart is." Megs said not taking her eyes off the shot she was pouring. "Was there someone?"

At first Sam did not understand what Megs meant. She was not even sure whether Megs was talking to her. But when Megs finally met her eyes she shook her head. "Not someone I could talk about."

Megs nodded almost imperceptibly.

"Besides, I struggle enough looking out for myself, let alone anyone else." Sam tried to laugh off the painful memories.

"Well, think about it. It might stop you needing to escape so much," Megs said as she skilfully filled the second tot glass to the brim.

Sam playfully rolled her eyes at Megs and grabbed the nearest shot. "Make that four tequilas." She smiled at Megs and downed the first two shots.

After Megs had poured the next two shots, Sam paid for the drinks and headed back over to where Pete was sitting, nursing his beer. She banged the two shot glasses on the table in front of him, took one and held it out in a wordless toast. He followed suit. They clinked glasses and downed the shots. Sam slowly replaced the glass on the table. As she looked up she caught Pete's unwavering gaze. Right there and then she made a decision. She cocked her head toward the door, got up and left. Pete did not need a second invitation and in a matter of seconds he followed her out of the bar.

The cottage bedroom was dark when they got there. Sam
entered first. She switched on the lamp next to the bed and
hung her jacket over the mirror stand while Pete waited,
watching her from the doorway.

Sam felt a little nervous. It had been a long time since she
had been intimate with anyone. But she needed this. She
craved the physicality of another human's touch; their
warmth, their energy, their passion. She needed to feel alive.
She needed to feel something.

She studied Pete for a moment as he leaned against the
door. He was a good looking guy. He was sweet, even
unassuming, and despite his persistent cocky advances in the
pub, she quite liked him. Sam was not a fool and knew,
judging by his behaviour, that he was quite used to getting
his way and probably had charmed his way into many a
woman's bedroom with those boyish good looks. She was also
pretty sure that he, like her, was just after the physical
gratification. Sam knew she had nothing emotional to give
right now and did not want the extra complications.

Sam slowly walked over to Pete, enjoying his expression
change from Boy Wonder to wolf. She came to a stop a few
inches from his chest and then leant forward and started to
kiss him, unbuttoning his shirt, sliding her fingers under the
fabric, enjoying the feeling of his warm flesh and soft body
hair under her fingertips. When he started to reciprocate by
pulling at her top, she grabbed his hands and led him to
the bed.

She unzipped his jeans and dropped them to the floor
around his ankles. He let her, content for her to take the
lead.

She pushed him backward to land on the bed.

She studied him in the low glow of the bedside lamp. He was lean and well-built, with milky white skin, smooth over toned muscles.

She undid her own jeans, and in one swift movement pulled them, and her underwear, down to the ground. She stepped out of them and got onto the bed, straddling him.

He tried to sit up to kiss her but she pushed him back down. Now was not the time for intimacy, she needed him rough and raw.

Her mind drifted as it always did, to Sabrina, always, Sabrina, until soon she felt like her being was overflowing with the bitter sweet memories. She leant back and started to stimulate herself in the way that she knew would make her come fast and hard, while she continued to ride him.

Within moments they both hurtled over the edge.

She collapsed forward with her hands on either side of his head. They were both wet with sweat, gasping, sucking in much needed air.

"God, we're so good together!" he finally said. "I've always known we would be."

Sam leaned down and kissed him chastely on the lips before she got up, grabbed her jeans and headed to the shower.

Pete sat up on his elbows and watched her leave. Then, with a contented smile he flopped back on the bed and dozed.

Ten minutes later she returned from the shower wrapped in a white towel. Pete sat propped up in her double bed, waiting for her. When he saw her enter the room, he smiled and patted the bed next to him, inviting her to come and join him.

Sam felt a little thrown by the gesture. She ignored it, stalling for time. She headed over to her cupboard. "There are fresh towels on the shelf if you'd like to clean up before you go." She cringed at the sound of her own voice. She did not mean for that to come out as cold as it did.

She took out a gown from the closet and wrapped herself in it before she let her towel slide from her body.

It took Pete a few seconds to register what she had said. "What?" He watched her intently, uncertain if he had understood correctly. When she did not say anything more and clearly made no move to join him in bed, there was no room for misunderstanding.

"You're serious?" he asked.

Sam inwardly braced herself before she turned back to face him. She went to sit at the bottom edge of the bed.

"Look, Pete, we both got what we wanted," she ventured gently.

Pete still looked uncertain.

"I mean, it was great! You were great!" Sam wanted him to feel good about what had just happened between them. "Thank you," she said, adding as much warmth to that one sentence as she could.

Pete was clearly at a loss for words. Sam assumed he was clearly accustomed to calling the shots and this was the last thing he had expected.

Finally, in a definitive move, he got up and gathered his

clothes from the floor. He was obviously bristling with hurt or anger. Without bothering to get fully dressed he headed to the door, where he stopped and glared back at her. He seemed about to say something but decided against it. He shook his head and disappeared into the darkness of the cottage.

Sam remained seated on the edge of the bed, not moving until she heard the sound of the front door close. She let out the breath she was holding. The cold night air folded in around her. She suddenly felt even more alone than she had before.

She got up and reached into her jacket pocket, retrieving the crumpled PhyCorp note. She collapsed onto the bed and considered the piece of paper.

Was that the right thing to do? To leave again so soon? Megs was her only family, the only person she had left. Was Megs right? What was she running from? Could she settle down and find a way to belong? Maybe not with Pete, but maybe there was someone else out there? Should she give village life a chance? She placed the PhyCorp advert on the night stand, turned off the lamp and stared into the darkness until finally sleep claimed her.

———————

Sam woke up feeling surprisingly refreshed for the first time since she had arrived back home. Despite being plagued by the usual fitful dreams, she had slept through until the morning. Perhaps the physical exertion and catharsis of her evening with Pete had done her some good after all. In fact, she was even in a reasonably good mood for a change.

Over coffee in the conservatory, she sat staring out at the lighthouse in the bay, contemplating her options.

Finally she made a decision: She was going to listen to her big sister for once. She was going to give this village a chance. She might even help out in the pub for a while and see how that felt. She resolved to head straight over to The Lighthouse Pub after a shower and give her sister the good news.

———

It was a little after noon when Sam entered the pub, a relieved and happy smile still stuck to her face.

Megs was in her usual position behind the bar pouring a draft of ale.

Just then Pete came through from the back room. When he saw Sam his step faltered and he stopped momentarily as if considering what to do.

She smiled at him, feeling a little sheepish. She knew it was bound to be a little awkward between them initially, as it sometimes is after a one night stand. Even so, the look of reproach on his face came as a bit of a surprise, and before she could say something, he skirted past Megs to the far side of the bar.

Sam stepped up to the bar counter. "What's up with him?" she asked Megs, hoping that there was more than just the events of the previous night to blame for Pete's mood.

When Megs finally turned towards her, Sam instantly knew something was very wrong. Megs had that cold fierce look in her eyes that Sam remembered from when they were children. It meant that Megs was no longer playing.

"Is it not enough that you only look out for yourself?" she said, her clipped, icy restraint slicing through Sam.

"What are you talking about?" Sam glanced from Megs to Pete and back again, trying to understand what was going on.

"You're not content being a miserable bastard by yourself, you have to ruin other people's happiness as well?" Megs said.

"I'm not sure what you're talking about—"

"Yes you do!" Megs said. "You're the 'reporter'. The so called 'observer', who is not that observant. Or perhaps you are, but just don't care."

"Megs. Really. What's going on?" Sam's mind was reeling in a desperate attempt to make sense of what the hell was going on. She hated seeing her sister so upset.

A long silence followed while Megs seemed to be contemplating how to continue.

"We were doing just fine until you came along." Megs said more softly, sounding quite deflated now that her initial anger had dissipated.

"Megs, seriously," Sam said more gently, "what are you talking about? What have I done?" When Megs did not answer Sam glanced over at Pete and then back at Megs. Suddenly realisation dawned; Megs was in love with Pete.

"Oh God, Megs, I'm so sorry! I didn't know... You said I should—"

"Not with Pete!" Megs banged a fresh glass on the counter.

Sam did not know what to say. What could she say?

"You know what? I'm glad we have the New State. At least it tries to stop people like you!"

Sam felt as if she had been thumped in the gut. For a

while she could not move, nor could she even think of anything to say. Her mind raced as she tried to make sense of how things could have taken such a wrong turn so quickly and so unexpectedly.

She was a fool to think she could do this, could settle for domestic bliss. She did not understand people. She was right, she was better off on her own away from everyone.

In that moment Sam made her decision. She dug her hand into her jacket pocket and pulled out the crumpled PhyCorp advert. She headed over to the pay-phone, lifted the receiver and dialled the number.

---

Back in her room in the little seaside cottage, Sam was getting ready to leave. She did not have much to pack, as she did not need much and most of her essentials were still in the duffle bag.

A sadness came over her as she pulled the white sheets back over the few items of furniture in her room. She was unsure of when, if ever, she would return.

The final item to be covered was the oval antique mirror she inherited from her Nan, along with the cottage and the lighthouse outside.

She paused in front of it and once again and assessed her reflection. She fingered the military dog-tags around her neck. She was no longer a soldier. But what was she now? Her eye caught the little lighthouse pendant, hanging from the mirror supports. The lighthouse, this cottage, was the closest she had been to having a home, a place of belonging. She grimaced at the irony. She felt like an emotional lighthouse, destined to be alone, on a rock, warning everyone to stay away.

She took off her dog-tags and swapped them for the lighthouse pendant. Even if she never returned, she would always be from here.

## 3

Shortly after the start of The War it became evident that the civilised world would require every bit of help, effort and luck in order to survive. All industry and commercial endeavours became focussed on supporting the war effort in every way possible. This new agenda propelled scientific research and technological advancement at a rapid rate, in all areas pertaining to out-doing, out-witting and out-fighting the enemy. However, it left very little in reserve to advance, replenish or even sustain the country, its economy and its people. Everyday life rapidly degraded into a rudimentary, grim existence.

Necessity being the mother of invention, people found, designed and created new ways to use old things to fit new purposes. The once highly commodified mobile or cell phone retained its coveted status, not so much as a phone, as there were no longer any operational domestic telecommunication networks, but for its plastic cover that could be melted down and reformed into bowls, cups and other useful tools around the home. Even vinyl records made a comeback, as raw material for crockery and other useful household implements and containers.

As part of the arms race, large and small research organisations worked tirelessly to out-bid and out-smart each other, in what had become a very small market. With the formation of the New State, these research organisations were granted operational autonomy. In this instance, heterogeneous diversity provided by independent endeavours, was favoured over the increased control of a unified enterprise under the military regime. However, as soon as any one of these organisations made a significant advance in science or technology which could benefit The State, the military muscled in and commandeered both the programme and the organisation.

PhyCorp was one of the few medium sized independent research organisation which, despite its successes, had so far resisted military takeover. It had achieved this by mostly staying under the military's radar—in fact, off everyone's radar. Its hidden location, deep below a deserted tin mine, nestled between water and land on an inhospitable stretch of the Cornish coast, went a long way to make that possible. Its success was also due to its good client-relationship management and the incredible reputation of the key researcher, Dr Victoria Henderson.

The company's long standing contract with the military to run a drugs testing programme for Class A and 2A non-lethal drugs provided a reliable, sustainable front. This deflected many questions and much speculation regarding the real research being conducted in the subterranean tombs. Rumour had it that PhyCorp was researching something that had the potential to bring about a sea change in the understanding of reality itself.

---

Sam stood in yet another long, slow moving queue leading up to a security checkpoint at the entrance to the main lobby of PhyCorp. She had already spent over two hours in a mammoth queue, outside in the freezing cold, where the preliminary applicant assessments and processing took place. While out there in the blustery weather, a hot beverage or two from an enterprising local vendor seemed like a marvellous idea. However, she soon regretted her decision when she realised that the nearest facilities were over two hours wait away.

There, up ahead, on the other side of the security checkpoint, she spotted a small sign to the "Restroom". She groaned inwardly. She considered asking someone to keep her place and then trying to convince the guard to let her through to use the facilities, but from what she had seen so far, goodwill was not high on the agenda amongst her fellow applicants, most of whom were obviously regular druggies looking for a free fix and a place to crash. As for the stern faced guards, she doubted whether her personal discomfort would matter to them.

Finally, it was her turn to pass through the security check. A short, stocky security guard in a black and blue uniform stepped forward and without a word started to manoeuvre her arms and legs as if he was arranging luggage on a conveyor belt. When he began to pat her down, a bit too thoroughly, she looked at him coolly, waiting for him to finish and make eye contact.

"I hope that was as good for you as it was for me," she said, calmly holding his gaze.

The guard's face flushed. "Next," he snorted.

---

Sam rushed straight for the Restroom. She barged through the door. Inside was another woman huddled over a basin. She got the distinct impression she had interrupted something but her need was greater at that moment. So she nodded and smiled briefly before she launched straight for the toilet cubicle.

When Sam finally came back out of the cubicle she was surprised to find the woman still standing in the same place. She smiled at her again and headed to the nearest basin. As she reached for the tap—

"No, no! Please, not that one," the woman said suddenly, her tone firm but earnest.

Sam smiled and moved off to another basin, assessing the woman in her peripheral vision. She was instantly struck by her self-assured manner and a sense of strength and confidence that surrounded her.

"Is something the matter?" Sam asked while she washed her hands. "Perhaps I can help?"

"Only if you have superpowers." The woman laughed quietly, clearly a little embarrassed.

Sam liked the sound. "Oh, I don't know. Give me a go."

The woman studied Sam for a moment, clearly assessing whether to let her into her secret.

"You don't know until you try," Sam added.

She noticed how beautiful the woman was. Her dark brown hair emitted a subtle auburn glow as it framed her chiselled features. She had dark eyes but she could not make out the exact colour. Sam realised that she was staring and looked away, feeling the heat rise to her cheeks.

"It's my ring," the woman finally said, a little frustration evident in her voice.

"Okay, I can definitely help with that," Sam said and immediately started to scan the floor.

"Sadly, it's not that simple!" The woman raised her brows and cocked her head to indicate a long, narrow, metal grate on the floor, under the basins, that covered a shallow drainage gutter.

"Ah. I see." Sam smiled, understanding. She bent down and carefully eased herself into the small space under the basins. She peered through the grate. There it was, glistening, a small, silver ring resting on white and dark marble pebbles.

She became aware of a presence next to her and realised the woman had also squeezed into the confined space.

Sam tried to lift the grate. It was fixed but with no obvious screws or latches to loosen.

She then tried to poke her finger down to reach the ring but after a couple of attempts she realised her fingers were just too short.

"I tried that too." The woman's soft voice seemed nearer than Sam had expected. "I'll have to call maintenance as I really don't want to lose my ring again."

Sam turned to talk to her and they bumped heads, almost accidentally kissing. Both of them recoiled, embarrassed. As Sam pulled back, reflexively bringing her hand up to her chest, her fingers grazed the little lighthouse pendant.

"I have an idea," she said and removed the pendant from around her neck. She held it in her hand like a little fishing line and then lowered it through the grate. Sam could feel the other woman move in closer. After only a couple of attempts, Sam managed to hook the ring with the thicker base of the lighthouse and lifted it steadily out of the water and up, carefully through the grate, to safety.

"Oh, that is brilliant!" the woman said, gently laying her hand on Sam's arm making her skin tingle under the touch. "Thank you so much!"

Sam studied the small silver signet ring for a moment. "No engraving?" she said as she dried it on her top before handing it over.

"No. Can't seem to settle on something that matters enough." The woman seemed suddenly shy.

As Sam handed her back her ring, their fingers touched. It was instantly electrifying, causing them both to start and their eyes to meet.

Emerald green, Sam thought.

Just then the door behind them opened and a woman Sam recognised from the queue outside entered and made a bee-line for the nearest cubicle.

The moment was ruptured. Instantly the woman next to Sam jumped up and switched on the hand-dryer, even though her hands were perfectly dry. Sam felt the physical loss of her nearness like a visceral chill, causing her to shiver. Not knowing what else to do, she got up and busied herself with tying her pendant around her neck.

Sam searched out the woman's eyes in the mirror. When their eyes finally met, the two of them shared a shy smile.

"Thank you," the woman mouthed over the noise of the dryer.

They held each other's gaze for a long moment.

Sam could feel her heart racing in her chest.

The toilet flushed in the nearby cubicle, thereby propelling the woman to turn and head out of the door, leaving Sam on her own to finish drying her hands and endure the awkward looks from the intruder.

I didn't even ask her name, Sam thought. She dashed out of the restroom but, by the time she emerged into the lobby, there was no sign of her mystery woman.

Once inside PhyCorp, it looked very much like any other large building that houses research activity such as this. If you really paid attention, you would eventually be struck by the absence of windows and the occasional, particularly narrow corridors or low ceilings where the subterranean rock could not easily be blasted away during construction. Otherwise, the halls and corridors were generally spacious and decorated in plain, pale colours complete with light vinyl floors and fluorescent day glow lights, giving it a distinct old hospital feel.

After her visit to the restrooms, Sam went to find the sample group she had been allocated to. She caught up with them as they were being escorted towards a locker room by a plump, stern looking orderly with tightly cropped, ginger curls.

Each participant was given a numbered tag and a two piece jumpsuit made from breathable synthetic material which, though close fitting, was thankfully not too excessively figure hugging, providing enough flexibility for physical activity and comfort.

"Some of you may know the drill, but that does not mean you should not listen," the orderly warned. "Place your clothes and personal possessions in a locker. They will remain there, ready for you to collect once you have been discharged after the trial." Her tone had a singsong quality that Sam guessed had come from having to give the same instructions week in and week out.

As she spoke, the orderly circled the room, checking that her instructions were being followed to the letter.

Diagonally across from Sam, a composed, athletic looking woman, whom Sam guessed might also be ex-military, shrugged out of her shirt and was about to pull on the jumpsuit, concealing her dog-tags, when the orderly pounced on her.

"Those have to come off." She pointed at the tags. "No personal identification is allowed during the trials." She glared and waited until the soldier had removed the tags.

Sam could see the turmoil on the soldier's face. Sam knew that feeling. Taking off those tags was literally the removal of the last vestiges of identity. During her time on The Front, those tags were often the only thing reminding her of who she was, and therefore, her purpose in the world. Sam watched the soldier remove the chain, kiss the tags and lay them down gently in her locker.

Sam picked an empty locker towards one corner of the room. She started hanging up her jacket. Next to her, a young blond woman barely in her twenties stood, arms folded nervously, fingering a locket around her neck as she glanced around the room. She let go of the locket abruptly when she realised Sam had seen her.

"Why no personal items?" She whispered to a slightly older, short haired brunette next to her.

The brunette waved her hand dismissively.

The orderly overheard her question and interjected. "Personal items can identify you. These are serious, anonymous trials."

Sam could see the young woman was still uncertain.

"Unless it has your name on it, it should be fine," Sam said quietly. The woman nodded, relieved, and tucked the locket into her top.

Sam's response had caught the attention of a striking dark-skinned woman who had wild, long black hair and a white streak in her fringe. There was something distinctly stallionesque about her. She and her petite younger companion with short white hair had, so far, been too absorbed kissing and canoodling on the other side of the room to take much notice of what was happening around them. Sam had first noticed them in the queue outside. They clearly made no effort to hide their intimacy, despite the illegality of their actions. The rest of the women, including the orderly, seemed not to mind or even pay much attention to them, probably because it would have been more trouble than it was worth. When she got caught watching them outside the woman with the streak had given her an unambiguous, mind-your-own-business look. Sam could feel her eyes on her, but she did not want a confrontation, or to be accused of staring.

"What kind of tests will they do, Jemma?" Sam heard the young woman next to her ask her companion.

"Don't worry about the tests, Jean, love," the brunette replied. Her face lit up as she winked and elbowed the younger woman. "Just focus on the trip," she said, followed by a deep, crackling smoker's laugh.

"What trip?" Clearly the new information did nothing to calm the younger woman's nerves.

"From the drugs... each time guaranteed." This elicited sudden whoops of excitement and appreciation from a huddle of women on the other side of Jemma.

"Yeah, why else do you think we do this?" a woman with a bright-red undercut said, giving her neighbour with matching coloured braids a high five.

Sam noticed how, whenever anyone spoke, they threw glances at the woman with the white streak. She was obviously their leader.

Jean looked even more nervous. Sam guessed that she was clearly new to the group and was not all that comfortable with their wayward ways.

For some reason, Sam felt compelled to put her mind at ease. "Don't worry, it's a placebo most of the time," Sam said softly.

"A what? What's that?" the young woman asked.

Unfortunately, the woman with the red braids had chosen that moment to pass by Sam, on her way to the basin, and overheard the conversation.

"Don't listen to her. What does she know!" the woman said, loud enough for everyone to hear. "She ain't a regular."

"What's up, Bee?" her companion with the undercut called out from across the room.

"This sister is saying they give us sugar pills, not drugs," the woman whipped her braids off her shoulder in a display of outrage.

"What? I've been on every rotation since last May and I never had no sugar pills," a shocked Jemma chimed. Sam noticed a number of furtive glances in the direction of their leader and her companion.

"Is that true? You sure they give us sugar pills?" the young woman asked Sam.

"No." Sam considered leaving her answer there, but then decided that the young woman deserved the truth. "However, it is quite likely. An organisation which spends billions on research will not want the unfortunate mixture of drugs to affect their results, let alone let their reliable control group become junkies. So if they have identified you as a regular they will most likely put you in the placebo sample most of the time."

"I thought they don't know our names or identity. So how would they know if we'd been here before?" Jean asked.

"Just because they don't know your name does not mean they don't have ways to identify you."

"Suz, you listening to this?" Jemma asked in the direction of their leader. "Is this true?"

"Is that true? You been selling me duds, Suz?" the woman with the undercut said.

Up to now the stallion and her companion had been entwined in a deep kiss, seemingly oblivious to the growing unrest around them.

Sam was surprised to see that it was the smaller, petite woman who ended their kiss and pulled away slightly, placing a finger on her taller companion's lips as she whispered a promise to be right back. She turned and headed towards Sam. Sam noticed her stallionesque girlfriend fold her arms and give Sam an almost rueful smile. The smaller woman was not as young as she had originally thought and in a few short strides she came to a stop, squaring up in front of Sam. This was a gesture that was almost comical, considering the difference in their stature, Sam's significant combat training and physically superior condition. Sam assessed it as nothing more than a flamboyant, theatrical display of showmanship and bluster, none of which she wanted to pander towards. She merely turned her back and continued putting her belongings into the locker.

In a flash, and with a loud crash of skull on metal, Sam felt her cheek connect squarely with the cold locker door as her legs gave way from a surprisingly strong blow to the back of her knees. She tried to brace her fall but found her hands in a vicelike grip behind her back as pain shot up her arms from the unnatural angle her thumbs had been wrenched into."

What the- Sam's thoughts were interrupted by the feeling of soft warm breath on her ear.

"Three important lessons for you, today, champ… One, never turn your back on a woman. Two, never underestimate someone due to their size. And finally, never stick your nose into my business again." The petite woman wrenched Sam's thumbs even further eliciting a painful groan. "Is that clear?"

Sam nodded, her cheek scraping against the rough vents on the locker door.

"It is rude not to answer a question when asked." The petite woman wrenched Sam's thumbs further.

The angle with which she had landed against the locker

meant it was difficult to speak. "Yes, it is clear," she forced the words out.

Her efforts must have appeased the small woman because Sam felt the pressure on her thumbs ease up. It was moments too late that she realised it was only the small woman's grip holding her up, preventing her from sliding unceremoniously down the locker and landing awkwardly on her knees, on the floor.

By the time Sam had recovered herself from the inelegant convoluted heap on the floor, the small woman was positioned in front of Jemma and had her hand around her neck pulling her forward leaning their foreheads together. Sam could hear her whispering soothing reassurances and she saw Jemma shake her head, swallow and then nod with childlike earnestness.

Sam watched as the petite woman then strolled over to the two women with the red braids and the undercut. She took them both by the neck in a similar fashion and then in turn pulled each one into a deep searing kiss. She whispered something to them to which they nodded. She then left them, throwing Sam a warning glance before she rejoined her tall companion to continue where they had left off.

---

The rest of the induction into the programme went surprisingly smoothly, after Sam made a conscious decision to stay clear of the petite blonde and her pack of followers. After a brief tour of the common areas in the facility, she found herself being led into a large room, which had three plain white walls and a large mirror covering the fourth. Men and women in lab-coats were busily tending to other test Subjects like herself, setting them up on various pieces of gym equipment scattered throughout the room.

Sam was directed to take her place next to a treadmill.

A young, earnest looking orderly, with a mop of curly dark hair and a fresh face greeted her politely.

"Ma'am, I need to set you up with the monitoring equipment," he explained as he fumbled awkwardly with the medical electrode pads. "Could you put your arms out to the sides, please?"

He tried to attach the electrodes to the various points on her torso.

After the third unsuccessful attempt Sam smiled to herself and glanced at his name badge. It read "Jesse Wyatte".

"You new here too?" Sam asked.

"Ah. No. Actually, been here a month," Jesse replied when he eventually realised Sam was talking to him.

"Just not had many female Subjects?" she said.

Jesse smiled shyly. "That obvious, huh?"

Sam returned the smile, trying to convey reassurance. "It might help if you think of me less as your girlfriend, and more like… an object."

Jesse's cheeks coloured and he gave a slightly relieved chuckle.

Moments later the electrode pads were all in place and Sam was ready to go. She stepped up onto the treadmill and Jesse hit the "GO" button starting her off on a warm up jog.

———

Behind the one way mirror that clad the entire fourth wall of the gym was a dark, narrow room, illuminated only by the partial light coming through the darkened glass and the unnatural blue-green glow from the screens and instrument panels inside. A number of lab-coated technicians busied themselves taking readings and monitoring the numerous instruments, while others worked together in small groups which were focussed on putting the Subjects in the gym through rigorous testing. One Senior Technician per group was kitted with a microphone and headset with which to communicate with the orderly in the gym who was working hands on with the Subject.

The Senior Technician assigned to Jesse and Sam's group was an older, balding man called Clive Trooney. "Push the gradient to max, clearly we have a tough one here," he commanded.

Inside the gym Sam was sweating and working hard but not over reaching. Her military background, and self-imposed fitness regime, ensured she was always in tip-top condition. However, despite Sam not showing any outward signs of discomfort, Jesse hesitated before slowly increasing the gradient.

"Orderly Wyatte, I said push the gradient to max," Clive Trooney bellowed in his ear.

Sam sensed that Jesse was sparing her so she smiled and winked at him to let him know she was okay.

Jesse adjusted the gradient and speed upward and Sam easily picked up the pace. She was quite enjoying the opportunity to stretch her legs after the long wait in the queues and the tension build up from the various selection processes. The fact that she passed all of them with flying colours did not alter the fact that she hated doing tests in the first place. That was something she should probably start getting used to if she was going to continue on in this place, she thought.

---

An hour later. "Give her five. Clearly it's going to be a long day," Clive Trooney's voice crackled in Jesse's ear.

Jesse hit the "STOP" button and Sam slowed down to a jog and then to a walk. Jesse passed her a towel to dry off while he checked his clipboard.

"Pretty impressive," he said.

"Since you've been staring at both equally long, I'm hoping you're referring to my stats, not my tits," Sam said keeping a straight face.

Jesse blushed profusely.

Sam broke the tension with a gentle punch to Jesse's shoulder and they both laughed. She enjoyed having someone to josh with. It had been a very long time. Jesse, although he was a bit older, reminded her of the youngest member of her Unit, Private Danny Tritton. He was barely eighteen and had the same sweet, caring nature. He had been like a little brother to her.

Jesse led her over to the water cooler where she took a long cool drink.

As she looked up she saw the main door to the gym open and in walked the beautiful brunette she had met in the restroom. Sam almost did not recognise her because she was now wearing a white lab-coat. Sam was instantly entranced by the memory of those captivating emerald eyes.

The woman headed over to the matronly orderly with the

cropped ginger curls who had been supervising their induction that morning. The orderly smiled broadly and handed her a clipboard. Sam watched as they conversed over the notes. Finally, the woman smiled that intoxicating smile and turned to head back to the exit.

Sam realised that her mystery woman was about to leave, so she grabbed Jesse's arm. "Who's that?" she asked, not taking her eyes off of her.

"Who?" Jesse was a little startled by the firm grasp of his arm, but he followed her gaze.

"Oh, that. That's THE Dr Victoria Henderson."

"Do you know her?"

"In my dreams!" Jesse stood shoulder to shoulder with Sam, sharing their unspoken admiration of Dr Henderson who had been stopped just in front of the door by another orderly showing her something in his file. "Sadly, only of her. She's the legendary genius behind this whole programme."

Sam grabbed Jesse's elbow and tried to drag him towards her quarry. "Take me to her."

"Whoa!" Jesse slipped his arm out of her grasp. "Which part of unattainable did you not understand? She doesn't tend to chit-chat to junior orderlies... or Subjects for that matter."

"Why?" Sam asked, distracted by Dr Henderson's grace and poise. Just then Dr Henderson threw her head back slightly and laughed at something the orderly said. Sam could not help smiling to herself. It must be wonderful to bask in that laughter.

"Well, mostly because she's pretty busy," Jesse said.

Sam was snapped back to the conversation but still kept her eyes glued to Dr Henderson.

"In any case, we don't see her around here much anymore." Jesse returned his attention to his clipboard to see what was next on the programme.

"Why's that?"

"She spends most of her time in maximum security, on the Advanced Programme."

Sam watched as Dr Henderson patted the orderly on the arm and headed out of the gym. Sam swallowed back her disappointment.

"What's that?" she asked returning her full attention to Jesse.

"For an ex-marine you certainly do ask a lot of questions."

"Some habits die hard." Sam was not about to explain her journalistic background. In fact, she thought it prudent to reveal as little as possible about herself while here. After all, she was only an anonymous research Subject. The last thing she wanted was to reveal anything personal that could allow PhyCorp or any other interested party to track her down in years to come.

"How does one get onto this Advanced Programme?"

Jesse chuckled until he realised she wasn't joking. "It's almost impossible. Rumour has it that the first guy who came near to passing all the selection trials got discharged before anyone could say 'pass me the clipboard'. A mate of mine saw him being dragged out muttering like a mad man that Aliens had abducted him. So, I know you don't just volunteer."

"Well, I just did." Sam looked Jesse straight in the eye to make sure he knew that despite their joshing, she was being serious.

**4**

Jesse wheeled Sam along a corridor of the maximum security area. The transfer into the ADV Programme took less time than Jesse had expected. It had been just under two weeks since Sam was first inducted into the Standard Programme. In the first instance he was astounded that her bold move to volunteer for the ADV Programme was even considered. Then again, her almost perfect test scores during the first seven days of induction must have had an effect on the decision to break protocol.

"I really don't need this." Sam said, referring to the wheelchair.

Jesse realised that being incapacitated must be somewhat alien for someone clearly used to being as active and in control as Sam seemed to be.

"If I was you I'd enjoy the pampering while it lasts," he said.

The corridors were quiet compared to the Standard Programme area. They turned down a section that had a number of large observation windows looking onto small individual laboratories. Inside there were people, probably Subjects, attached to sensors and wires connecting them to various monitoring equipment. There were a number of lab technicians and orderlies hovering around in each lab, tending to the Subjects and recording data from the beeping monitors.

In one of the labs an alarm suddenly sounded. This was followed by a flurry of technicians and orderlies rushing to hold a convulsing Subject down on the gurney.

Sam and Jesse watched as one of the technicians prepared a syringe cartridge and after a substantial struggle, eventually managed to inject the Subject. It took a few minutes before the Subject finally calmed down and collapsed back onto the gurney, unconscious.

Once all the orderlies had backed off and released the Subject, Sam noticed that the technician who had injected the man was still holding the man's hand. He was gently stroking his thumb across the back of his hand as he watched him relax into a deep slumber.

"You sure you're up for this?" Jesse asked.

Sam ignored the question choosing instead to take a long look at the technician. He was a young man, Sam guessed in his early thirties. He held his head drooped forward so that his shoulder length straight blond hair fell forward creating a curtain, obscuring most of his face.

"BP is stabilised, sir," one of the orderlies advised the young technician, which seemed to snap him out of his trance. He lowered the Subject's hand, and in a well-practiced reflex, his own hand shot up to secure the stray lock of hair behind his ear, revealing more of his beautiful fine chiselled features.

Sam had not really thought about what she would be letting herself in for by volunteering for the ADV Programme. All she knew was that she wanted to see Dr Henderson again. Now the magnitude of her foolhardy leap was starting to register. Was she up to it? Did she have what it took? What would it take? She thought back to her time in the War Zone and her Unit. Surely this could not be any worse than what she had to endure back then? At least here she did not have anyone she cared about or anyone who placed their trust in her—nobody to let down. She should have died back then. She was on borrowed time now anyway, so she had nothing to lose.

Sam was about to comment on this when she heard Jesse behind her. "Martin? Martin Monroe? Is that really you?"

Sam watched as the blonde technician looked up, at first surprised to hear his name being called. Then his face lit up when he saw Jesse. "Jesse Wyatte!" He made his way out of the lab towards them. "Wow! What brings you here?"

They shook hands.

"I started working for PhyCorp a few weeks ago and this here is my first ADV Subject." Jesse pointed at Sam. "Martin, meet Sam."

Martin smiled down at Sam as he gently shook her outstretched hand.

"He and I go way back," Jesse explained. "When I was a trainee nurse he was on a pre-med rotation at the hospital I was working at." Jesse turned his full attention back to Martin. "What are you doing here? Thought you swore you would never lay hands on a live patient and were going to take the academic route to a PhD and then researcher?"

"Yeah well... best laid plans..." Martin shrugged.

"What happened? How have you been? How's Charles? You guys still in touch?" Jesse bubbled over with questions.

Martin nodded but Sam could detect a seriousness had come over him. She noticed him glance round the lab and corridor briefly before answering.

"I am still with Charles. Sadly, he's not well."

"Ah sorry, man!" Jesse said. "Is it serious?"

Martin shrugged. "The inevitable." A sad smile lined his thin lips.

Jesse nodded.

"So I am just staying under the radar and trying to earn enough to pay for his meds."

"Can you not get them based on your involvement here?" Jesse asked.

Martin shook his head. "Too dangerous. So we have to go the state health route."

"Ah man! Really sorry to hear that! That must be tough."

"Anyway, look at you." Martin attempted to lighten the mood. "You've filled out."

Sam could see Jesse blush at the compliment.

"And this is your first ADV Subject?" Martin asked. "You're her P.C.A?"

Jesse nodded.

"Where are you headed?" Martin asked, starting to walk.

Jesse studied the clipboard. "Lab N.C. fourteen."

Martin looked surprised. "Wow, so you are the new Volunteer."

Jesse shoved the clipboard into the back pocket of the wheelchair and pushed it to catch up with Martin.

"I guess so," Sam said.

"Well they've assembled a special little team for you.

Luckily I'm on it." Martin smiled and then turned his attention back to Jesse. "I have to report to my supervisor before, but I will see you at the lab a little later."

"Okay. Great. See you there."

"Oh, and Jess," Martin's voice dropped to a low whisper. "You won't—"

"Of course not!" Jesse replied swiftly, giving Martin a reassuring smile.

Martin nodded relieved. He squeezed Jesse's shoulder in a gesture of gratitude and headed off.

"He seems rather nice." Sam added a little tease by raising her eyebrows playfully to suggest there might have been be a little more than friendship between the two men.

Suddenly Jesse bent down in front of her. "Shhh!" he hissed looking around the corridor to see if anyone would have heard. "You can't say that!" His voice still a serious whisper.

"I was only joking, who is going to mind here?—" Sam whispered back.

"Just please don't. Even an innocent joke can have dire consequences! This place has ears, like any other, and the same rules apply. State trumps science any day."

"Okay, I'm sorry," Sam said simply, genuinely regretting her comment.

Jesse seemed satisfied with her apology.

He got up and began to push the wheelchair once more.

"For the record," he said, "he's my friend."

Sam nodded, admiring how much he seemed to care about others.

"This is it," Jesse said as he slowed the wheelchair down near a solitary door on a shorter, more secluded corridor.

The door had a small round vision-panel on the top half. Unlike the other labs they saw earlier, this one did not have an observation window through which one could see the interior from the corridor.

Jesse stepped around the wheelchair and turned the door handle, pushing the door open to reveal a dark room beyond. He wedged the door and pushed Sam inside a couple of feet where he engaged the wheelchair brakes and began to search the nearby wall for a light-switch.

Sam got up out of the wheelchair and slowly stepped farther into the room.

Once inside, Sam noticed a distinct electronic buzz and an eerie, dark-blue fluorescent glow emanating from what looked like high tech instrument panels. Three out of four walls were lined with cabinets filled with science and medical apparatus. A few feet in front, a large dark object obscured her view of the far side of the room.

Jesse finally found the light-switch and flicked it on.

Three large day-glow spotlights blinded them both. When she could open her eyes again, she saw the spotlights converged on a monstrous multi-configuration chair, elevated on a round raised platform, like a stage holding prime position in the centre of the room.

The fourth wall consisted of a bank of six flat screens, directly in front of the chair.

Sam slowly took a few more steps into the room, and as she did, she realised that the third wall to her side nearest to the door, was in fact a large floor-to-ceiling mirror, reflecting back the entire room, including the monstrous chair, and making the moderate-sized lab look twice as large.

Sam headed over to the chair. She was about to reach out and touch the smooth material of the armrest when she was startled by a noise behind her. She spun round to catch a brief glimpse of a compact figure as he pushed on through a door just inside the Lab entrance, which Sam had not noticed before. She deduced that, like the gym she had been in before, this lab had its own Observation room behind the mirrored wall.

She caught sight of her small reflection next to the formidable looking chair.

A filtered, clipped, voice echoed over an intercom, startling her slightly. "Orderly Wyatte, please get the Subject set up in the chair."

Jesse appeared next to Sam in the halo of bright light surrounding the chair. Wordlessly he helped her get into it. He then pulled over a metal trolley carrying an E.C.G. monitor with accompanying sensors and electrode pads. It was similar to the one in the gym, except there seemed to be a lot more sensors. He smiled reassuringly at her before he gently positioned the electrode pads on her temples, chest and abdomen.

Sam did her best to return the smile and hide her nerves. For some reason, which seemed odd under the circumstances, she did not want Jesse to worry.

Then suddenly a man appeared behind Jesse, stepping into the light. He was a short man with a humourless, puristic scientist look about him. He wore thick, dark rimmed glasses and had an unnaturally thick head of neatly trimmed white grey hair.

Without so much as an introduction, he adeptly injected Sam's arm with a bright orange liquid. The site of the injection stung.

"Christ! Not even a hint of foreplay," Sam checked his name badge, "Dr Elms." She gritted her teeth against the pain. "You must do great with the ladies."

"The Subject needs to know that this is a colourant to enable the monitoring of neural and cognitive activity in the brain," Dr Elms addressed Jesse, avoiding eye contact with Sam. He then reached into his pocket and brought out a chunky transparent ring which he handed to Jesse. Inside the ring was a thin vein of oily purple liquid, like ink.

"As the Personal Care Assistant for this Subject, if the Subject were to experience an abreaction at any point, it is your duty to administer the tranquilliser instantly by punching it directly onto the skin. That way no one will get hurt."

Jesse studied the ring and then gingerly slid it onto his middle finger.

"The sensors attached to the head and body are acutely sensitive, so the Subject needs to remain perfectly still." Dr Elms started to pace around the chair. "We do have restraints, for the Subject's safety and comfort, however, Dr Henderson insists we offer the Subject the choice to exercise self-control… initially anyway."

"Good, I prefer not to jump straight to bondage on a first date," Sam quipped.

Sam felt unsure whether Dr Elms was in fact walking around the chair or whether the room had started to spin. She squeezed her eyes closed to try to focus her vision.

"If at any point the exercises become too strenuous or the

Subject wants to stop, she just needs to press this red button." Dr Elms pointed to a red button on the armrest about an inch to the outside of Sam's hand.

"Beats having to remember a safe word," Sam said.

"If she does, the tests will immediately be discontinued. She will be given a hot cup of tea and discharged from the programme with the remuneration as agreed. Is that understood?" For the first time Dr Elms looked directly at Sam and met her gaze, waiting.

She nodded and swallowed, her throat suddenly very dry. "One strike and you're out. Right. I get it."

Dr Elms gave one firm nod and disappeared back into the dark.

Suddenly, the bank of screens in front of Sam flickered to life as a large PhyCorp logo appeared as one image across all six screens. "Science to rebuild an empire," a man's voiceover echoed through the room. The screen suddenly went blank and then a few seconds later the image of a bright red apple with a single large bite taken from it on a pure white background filled the screen.

"I want the Subject to view the following set of images," Dr Elms' voice boomed over the intercom.

Sam put her head back and readied herself for whatever was to come.

## 5

Earlier that morning Dr Elms doorstepped Victoria at the entrance to her office to report on the new Subject's progress. He was very excited, as excited as the sober Dr Elms could be, over the fact that she had passed the Preliminary test phase of the ADV Programme, and as a result, he was eager to have her start on the Class One trials that day.

Victoria was a little sceptical. From a field of over sixty extremely high functioning Subjects, who had undergone the Preliminary phase, not one had shown anywhere near the required aptitude to progress onto the Class One trials. In fact, she had begun to wonder if it was possible for anyone to pass the Preliminaries, let alone get through to the final stages of her programme. Privately she had been preparing herself to rethink the whole ADV Programme. Still, if this Subject had so much potential, it was a rare opportunity to test that part of the process and protocols, even if she had to redesign the Programme.

Unfortunately, she had been summoned to a meeting with Director Morten and the Board that morning, where she had to justify her past quarter's expenditure. Knowing, that after a string of recent failures, the entire organisation was desperate for some positive results and that progress could not be delayed, she instructed Elms to start on the trials without her.

Directly after her meeting, Victoria headed down to the Lab. She was keen to see how Dr Elms and his team were getting on. It was hard, sitting through all that negativity in the Board meeting and not spilling the beans on their new Subject's preliminary success, but Victoria knew all too well that sharing unratified good news was even more likely to lead to career suicide than constant underachievement, neither of which formed part of her career plan.

She entered the Observation room quietly, nodding briefly at Martin Monroe and Anthony Phillips who were the two gifted scientists she had recruited onto Dr Elms' team.

She swiftly assessed the current activity and was perplexed to see that they were still engaged in the initial stages of the Class One programme. She had expected them to have either aborted the trials if the Subject had not been successful, or progressed much further by now.

"Dr Elms, is it all going well?" she asked.

Dr Elms spun around, slightly startled. Most of the time he reminded her of a neatly turned out gerbil, especially when he had his spectacles perched on the end of his nose, however on this occasion he looked uncharacteristically confused.

"Yes, ma'am," he said speaking faster than normal, "the Subject appears to be slightly more resilient than expected." He handed her a computer tablet displaying a series of tabular scores and graphs illustrating the Subject's Class One test results so far.

It took Victoria a while to get used to being called "ma'am". It was especially troublesome to her in the early years, when she was fresh out of university, given that all her colleagues were much older than she was. She found the term alienating and quite pretentious. She soon realised that such a formal salutation was not only a way to show her respect but a necessary reminder to her colleagues that her youth was not reflective of her acumen and status. She also realised that it helped create a necessary distance between her and her colleagues and peers. It served as a reminder to her that, as much as she had wished otherwise, she would never fit in with these people. She was different and would always be different. So rather than resist, and put herself and them through further awkwardness, she decided to accept it, and kept pretty much to herself.

"I see", she said as she scanned the data. The scores were very impressive, but there was a problem.

"And you have administered the T.D.?" she asked.

"Of course, ma'am. Four applications of the truth drug and three doses of the resistance inhibitor so far. She should be an open book ma'am." Dr Elms nervously poked at the bridge of his glasses.

"Dr Monroe, what is your psychological assessment of the Subject?" Victoria asked.

Martin Monroe cleared his throat and tucked a rebellious lock of hair behind his ear. "Ma'am, there seems to be no obvious psychological inhibitors or contra-indications and, so far, the trial procedures have been pretty standard."

Victoria turned to Anthony. "And you, Dr Phillips? Any

thoughts?"

Anthony was a seemingly relaxed big dude, always in jeans and a T-shirt under his too small lab-coat. He had a juvenile passion for computer games and comics and a perpetual octagonal indentation of the back end of a Biro just above his left eyebrow. However, Victoria knew him to be a devoted husband, father of two young boys and a man with a mind the size of planet. She recruited him for his big, technical brain and his soft heart. He had helped her, almost single-handedly, programme all the software that underpinned the institution and the ADV Programme.

"No ma'am, I have quadruple checked and all systems are fully functional and reporting correctly," Anthony said.

"Okay, continue," she said handing Dr Elms back the computer tablet.

Victoria was very conscious of the risks involved in administering T.D.s and inhibitors, combined with subjecting anyone to the extreme levels of stimuli that this part of the trial required. But, she constantly reminded herself that in the interests of science, if you didn't push the boundaries you would never break them. After all, every Subject who entered her programme knew the risks and they were greatly rewarded for their sacrifice. Besides, although most of them had some personal reason for signing up, they were all rigorously evaluated as 'suitable' prior to the trials. This was their last chance to do something good for the "civilised world".

Even though she knew it was not very scientific, she wondered who this impressive new Subject could be. She stepped up to the one-way glass to look into the Lab.

From the awkward angle of the chair on the platform it

took her a few seconds to recognise the woman who lay there… her!

No, it couldn't be! It was the woman from the restroom. Suddenly Victoria felt a tingle of panic spider along her forehead.

What was she doing here? There must have been some mistake. "This subject is supposed to be in the Day Programme." Victoria grabbed the computer tablet to see the Subject's number.

"Yes, Ma'am, she transferred in from there." Dr Elms replied, looking slightly uncomfortable.

"Transferred in?" Victoria asked, trying to remain outwardly calm and suppressing the alarm bells chiming in her head.

"Yes," Dr Elms glanced down at his paperwork. "I believe she is a volunteer."

"The volunteer—" Victoria said.

"Yes, ma'am. She scored exceptionally highly in the Day trials, so when she asked to be part of the ADV Programme, you agreed to allow it. A very wise decision I might add. Have a look at her Prelim scores, Ma'am. She is by far the best candidate we've seen," Dr Elms said hurriedly, like a child trying to prevent his Christmas toy from being taken away by his parents.

Victoria studied the test scores as a means of giving herself a few much-needed seconds to regain her composure.

"These are her psych and physicals?" Victoria clarified. They were incredibly high. She did remember that Dr Elms had consulted her about a Subject in the Day Programme who had done exceptionally well and had volunteered for the ADV Programme. She had stupidly formed a very prejudiced image of who the ex-marine might be. She inwardly chided herself for that. She, of all people, should know better than to make assumptions. Assumptions are an inherent human shortcut and nothing more than intellectual laziness.

Nevertheless, she was the last person Victoria would have imagined as her new rising star.

"Have all the terms and conditions been explained to her in detail?" she asked.

Dr Elms nodded.

"So she knows exactly what she has signed up to?" Victoria glanced at Anthony and Martin for confirmation. Although they both nodded, she could see they were both holding their breath, fearing what the outcome of this questioning might be.

"Very well," she finally said. "But, we need to be very thorough on the paperwork because she is a volunteer and has not been vetted and approved like the rest. If, at any point, she shows even the slightest sign of an abreaction she needs to be released with proper care and rehabilitation."

"Of course, Dr Henderson." Dr Elms nodded.

Victoria again glanced at Anthony and Martin who nodded too.

She turned back to observe the Subject. "So what seems to be the problem?"

"Ma'am, her neural response scores are off the charts. Her creative index is phenomenal and so far, in all but one category, she seemingly has the moral fibre of a saint," Dr Elms said.

"There must be a reason why the Class One trials are taking so long." Victoria studied the woman in the chair for a long moment.

"It's her trigger, ma'am." Dr Elms admitted. "We have not been able, as yet, to isolate her trigger. So far, the results have been inconclusive."

Victoria found herself playing with the ring on her finger as memories of their meeting in the restroom rushed back. She had not felt an instant connection like that with anyone in a very long while. At the time, and for some time afterwards, it made her feel almost giddy. She had not been able to stop thinking about her and wondering who she was and what she was doing at the institute. Initially she had hoped that she was one of the new staff members and perhaps they might meet again. Finally her curiosity got the better of her and she made some enquiries. That was when she saw her in the gym that day on the treadmill. She was gutted and gave up all hope of ever seeing her, let alone talking to her, again. Never in a million years had she foreseen her lying here, in the Lab, as an ADV Subject.

Victoria took a deep breath. Whatever flight of fancy that little encounter had started, it was now irrefutably obliterated. Come what may, she was a scientist, a professional. The research and her professional protocols came first. That was the vow she had made to herself the day she graduated. Not to mention, she was now her Subject with all the ethical rules and responsibilities that entailed.

At around 17:45 hours Victoria realised they had been at it for hours and everyone, including the Subject, must be nearing complete exhaustion. "Okay, I think you gentlemen have done enough for one day. After this set let the Subject get some rest and we'll start afresh tomorrow morning." Victoria turned and left the Observation room.

Dr Elms had also left shortly after Dr Henderson, leaving Jesse, Martin and Anthony Phillips to finish up for the night.

After annotating and backing up the data, Anthony went into the Lab to power down the instruments, leaving Jesse and Martin alone in the Observation room. Jesse decided that was a good time to ask the question that had bugging him since the start of the trials on the ADV Programme.

"What are you guys trying to do with Sam?"

Martin glanced up at him, pausing a few moments while obviously considering Jesse's question. "It's Classified, Jess," he finally answered.

Jesse held his breath and waited, hoping that Martin would change his mind.

Martin's expression softened. "Okay, but you didn't hear it from me. The primary hypothesis is that the human brain has a latent ability to manifest thoughts in the real world."

Jesse was confused. He realised that it would be a real shame to be let into such a big secret but still be none the wiser because he was unable to understand it.

"You've heard people say that we only use 10% of our brains?"

Jesse nodded.

"Well, we believe that to be true. We also believe that the other 90% has a latent potential that could be used to interact with the world, other humans and species."

"You mean like mind over matter?"

"A bit. It's unclear whether one person's manifestations, if they are even possible, would actually materialise or merely alter the observer's perceptions," Martin said.

"You mean like telepathy?" Jesse asked.

Just then movement in the Lab caught both Jesse and Martin's eye. Anthony was on his way back so Martin sped up.

"Yes, in simple terms like a telepathic projection, which seems more likely than the mind actually having the ability to physically alter the molecular structure of energy and matter."

Jesse felt as if he was in a sci-fi movie. "Wow!"

Martin nodded and smiled good-naturedly. "Glad you asked now?"

"This seems huge!"

"Yes, it could change our fundamental understanding of reality." Martin continued, clearing his desk.

Anthony entered the Observation room and Jesse took that opportunity to slip back out into the Lab to tend to Sam and escort her to her new quarters. Unlike on the Day Programme where everyone slept in bunk beds during the short trials, on the ADV Programme the Subjects were allocated their own rooms.

Jesse wheeled Sam down the hall to her room. Earlier that day he had gone to inspect it, to make sure that it was suitably equipped with blankets, towels, bedclothes and everything she could possibly need during the night. This would be her first night in segregated sleeping quarters. She was now regarded as a high profile Subject. What that translated into was that she was now a multi-million pound asset and it was his job to make sure nothing happened to her. He had been instructed to lock her in her room overnight. This was part of his job he was not at all comfortable with, but he had to follow orders, for his sake as well as Sam's. He did understand that the institute could not really afford to have valuable Subjects wandering off in the middle of the night, but it still felt a little too much like incarceration. So, he had resolved, in his own way, to compensate by making sure that she had everything she could possibly want in the room, and hopefully there would be no need to venture out anywhere. He hoped that perhaps she might not even realise that she was locked in.

He noticed that Sam had been very quiet since they left the Lab. This was not unexpected, considering how exhausted she must be after the day she had had.

He opened the door and pushed the wheelchair into the sparsely furnished little room. It had a single metal slab with a thin mattress as a bed, wedged between two large instrument panels. There was a tiny basin with a small square mirror above it and a toilet beyond it in the corner. Cupboards or any normal bedroom furniture were deemed redundant since she had no belongings or clothes other than the high tech breathable suits and underwear the Institute provided.

At first, Jesse did not realise Sam had spoken. "Was she there?" Sam asked again.

Even on hearing her question he was not clear what she meant. Then he remembered why she joined the programme in the first place – Dr Henderson. He nodded and started to make her bed with the sheets and blankets he had brought in earlier.

"She is truly amazing. She has a mind like a steel trap and

it's not surprising everyone respects her so much. She is gentle and kind and—" As he turned back he saw Sam trying to stand up out of the chair. She was teetering dangerously close to collapsing.

"Whoah!" He grabbed her and helped her get settled on the bed.

"You sure you are up to this?" Jesse began to worry that entering the ADV Programme had been a terrible mistake. "Why do you want to do this so badly?"

"I could ask you the same question." Sam said. "You are here almost all the time, even when you don't need to be."

He had to admit that Sam was far more perceptive than her somewhat flippant façade would lead one to believe. When they first met he mistook her for a jock, but he soon realised that she had much more to her than met the eye. The qualities that were instantly apparent were impressive, such as her physical strength, agility and, sometimes slightly crude, wit. These aspects diverted perception from her depths.

In order to dodge her prying eyes he headed to the basin to pour her a glass of water.

"What else could I do that's useful? I'm not a soldier, I'm not a farmer and I'm not super bright but I do enjoy helping people; so, I studied nursing…"

When he turned back he found Sam fast asleep, slumped on top of the half made bed. He took pity on her and covered her gently with a blanket. He watched her sleep for a few moments before he left and then locked the door quietly behind him.

He made a mental note to be there early enough the next morning to unlock her door before she awoke.

## 6

Victoria entered the Observation room carrying a blue folder. She nodded hellos to the three scientists.

From his position, seated out of the way against the glass, Jesse had seen Dr Henderson come in through the door next to him. He had expected her to treat him pretty much how he had been treated by the other three men – as if he was invisible. He did not take it personally. He understood they were scientists working on a very important project and he was the P.C.A. It was not that he felt his job was in any way less important, just different. If he was being honest, he preferred not to be engaged in other things too much, because that would distract him from keeping a watchful eye on Sam. The last thing he had expected was for Dr Henderson to talk to him.

"It's Jesse Wyatte, I believe," she stretched out her hand towards him.

Jesse jumped to his feet and shook her hand. "Yes, Dr Henderson. It's Jesse, just Jesse."

Victoria smiled at him. It was not often one found a genuine non-arrogant person in her line of work.

"You are Sam's P.C.A., I believe," she asked.

"That I am, ma'am." Jesse liked the way Dr Henderson used Sam's first name and had not referred to her as the Subject.

"Please could I ask you to complete a Psych Eval Report daily on her mental state and just leave the file in the rack when you're done," she said.

He nodded and took the file.

"Thanks." She gently squeezed his shoulder. "It is very important that you keep a close eye on her as the trials progress. She will need someone in her corner to make sure she is coping and ensure she is being looked after."

Jesse nodded again, suddenly feeling as if he had been assigned to be the President's personal guard.

Victoria turned back to the rest of the observation room. "Status, please?" she said.

"We've completed all grade two fear stimuli," Dr Elms said as he handed her the computer tablet.

"And?" She studied the results.

From his tone she could tell that it was not going to be good news. She did not like this batch of tests in the first place and didn't believe a usable trigger could ever be established from fear responses. Fear made people unpredictable.

"Still nothing, ma'am. Should we advance to grade three?" Dr Elms asked.

"No, Dr Elms. You know I don't like the use of excessive negative stimuli."

"Yes, ma'am," he said as if he had forgotten.

Victoria handed him back the tablet.

"Has the Subject had her first T.D. today yet?" Victoria asked.

"Yes, ma'am, but the next injection of the truth drug is due in a few minutes, ma'am," Martin replied.

Victoria nodded, took a deep breath and headed into the Lab.

Victoria strode up to the Subject's chair.

"Hello. My name is Dr Henderson." She offered Sam her hand, conscious that Sam might not be expecting to see her. She wondered if Sam would recognise her from their first meeting. Don't be silly Victoria, it is probably only you who remembers that meeting as anything out of the ordinary. For all you know she might often help complete strangers fish their nondescript pinky rings out of drainpipes.

"So I'm told." Sam smiled, taking Victoria's hand seemingly unfazed at seeing Victoria again, until Victoria felt the little subtle squeeze Sam delivered as part of her handshake. She does recognise me.

Victoria suddenly became acutely aware of the cool soft hand in hers. She had to resist the powerful urge to run a thumb over the smooth surface of her skin.

"You seem to be a woman of many talents." Victoria inwardly cringed at her clumsy reference to their first meeting.

"Thank you," Sam said, still not letting go of Victoria's hand. "Not half as many as you, I hear."

Victoria felt even more flustered by the slightly flirtatious compliment and she retracted her hand, quickly busying herself with loading the T.D. syringe cartridge.

"Does that mean you'll be taking an interest in my case from now on?" Sam asked.

"I will be supervising your progress, yes." Victoria tried to steer the conversation back to the more professional realm.

As Victoria took hold of Sam's arm to inject her, she was again slightly startled by how smooth and soft her skin felt. She noticed her own hands trembling slightly. As she injected Sam, Sam grunted softly from the sting of the injection which sent an unexpected thrill down Victoria's spine.

"Good, I'd hate to be doing this for nothing," Sam said.

The comment snapped Victoria back to reality. For a moment she was not sure what Sam meant but she caught herself before she actually asked. She had resolved to maintain a professional, objective distance from her Subjects, especially this one.

"If there is anything you need… just ask Jesse. His sole purpose as your P.C.A. is to make sure you are as comfortable as possible throughout your time with us."

"I'll do my best, Doc." Sam smiled.

Victoria did not miss the look Sam gave her, the way her eyes just dipped a little too low suggesting a more intimate rapport between them. Even though she was trying to maintain clear professional boundaries, she could not help giving Sam's arm a gentle reassuring squeeze before she turned and headed back into the Observation room.

Once inside she was fully back to business.

"Martin, I want you to load the full Affirmation sets A to F," Victoria instructed.

"Yes, ma'am."

"Anthony, I want hard copy printouts of all bio, E.C.G. and output feeds to the printers."

"Yes, ma'am." Anthony immediately turned to load the printers with new reams of paper.

"Okay. Let's begin." Victoria turned her attention to her Subject.

---

Four hours later, the team, including Victoria, was still hard at work monitoring Sam's responses to various sets of stimuli. Knowing how hard Victoria worked, the whole team was keen to pull their weight. This resulted in them all skipping lunch, choosing to eat as they worked. Even Jesse who did not have very much to do other than observe Sam chose to stay in his seat near the glass and keep vigil in case he was needed.

Suddenly, the door to the Observation room flew open and in burst Director Hugo Morten. He was a man in his late forties, dressed in a natty, executive light green suit. To those who did not know him he came across as a lean, light-footed dandy and was often assumed to be a closet homosexual, however most of the women in his office knew otherwise.

"I hear we have found our star," Director Morten announced.

Victoria cringed internally. She had hoped to keep this news off his radar until they had at least established a usable trigger.

"A little too early to tell, Director," she said continuing to focus on the results as they came in.

"I hear she's spanking the tests. The best Subject to date by far," he pressed on undeterred.

Victoria wondered who had been the bearer of the great news. "Yes. That might be true but—"

"So what's the problem?" Director Morten had a penchant for over simplification. He always wanted to boil things down to their bare essence—black or white. In fact he often encouraged his staff to boil their issues or complaints down to a single sentence. "Simple things are easy to solve," he would say. Although that was a truism, Victoria was not sure he understood the reductionist implications.

"I want the good news." Director Morten rested one hand on his hip while the other subconsciously stroked the silk tie against his chest.

Victoria had worked with Morten for years. She knew he prided himself on his great managerial and motivational skills. Sometimes, however, she thought he came across more like a cheerleader than the Director of a prestigious research institute. But, it was not her place to give him feedback. Besides, he did what he did best and usually left her to do her job—a mutual understanding that had allowed a, mostly non-acrimonious, working relationship to exist between them for over a decade.

Victoria took a few steps closer to the one-way glass so she had a better view of Sam.

Director Morton too stepped closer.

"We still have no idea what motivates or drives her,

Director," Victoria explained. "So far our tests remain inconclusive."

Morton began to pace behind her, rubbing his hands together.

Victoria had to fight hard to resist the instinct to raise her eyes to the ceiling. Did he really think in a room with three of the most accomplished brains in the country, he would solve the puzzle that had been confounding them for days?

Suddenly he stopped. "Have you tried sex, Dr Henderson?"

Victoria was thrown. "I beg your pardon!" She was no stranger to Morten's persistent advances over the years, but they were usually limited to moments in his office or other relatively private spaces. She surmised he did not want to risk being rejected in public, let alone in front of his employees.

"Libido, Dr Henderson." Morten continued to explain, oblivious to the reason she could possibly be fazed by such a proposition. "I believe the sex drive is a very fertile ground for motivation."

"Yes, Director." Victoria recovered herself quickly. "Basic drives can be powerful motivators. Thank you. We'll make sure to cover that."

"Good." Morten looked very pleased with himself. "Whatever it is, I look forward to some real results soon. I'll expect a report on my desk daily."

"Dr Elms, have we tracked all the results on The Auditor so far?" Victoria asked.

Dr Elms went over to check a small black box whose sole purpose was to record all data from the various CCTV cameras that kept vigil over the main Lab space and collect all data streams from all the various monitoring instruments.

It was Anthony who designed it and had affectionately named it 'The Auditor'. The name stuck.

"Yes, ma'am. The Auditor's in place," Dr Elms said. Then, surprising Victoria, he addressed Morten directly. "We'll have the first report on your desk by the end of the day, sir."

This seemed to satisfy Morten, who turned on his heel and left.

---

It was close to 18:00 hours. Jesse entered the Observation room with a tray of coffees. The team looked tired.

Dr Elms stood poring over the desk of printouts they had collected earlier. "What are we missing? I've just flooded her senses with probably the most diverse range of erotic stimulants available for," he checked his watch, "two hours straight."

"Yeah, and in the process completely over-stimulated ourselves to the point of desensitisation," Anthony quipped. "Not sure how I'm going to explain that to my wife tonight. She's already struggling enough with just the two boys as it is."

Martin and Jesse sniggered.

Victoria looked up from her computer screen. "Let's see."

Anthony looked up completely shocked and rapidly turned scarlet until he realised Victoria was speaking to Dr Elms.

This caused another snigger to come from Jesse and Martin.

Dr Elms handed Victoria the E.C.G. printouts. They

were both too focussed to pick up on the humour she had caused.

"More or less a complete flat-line. No more than a 10% increase in libidinal response." Dr Elms rubbed his eyes behind his glasses.

"Anthony, you did load the full set?" Victoria asked.

"Yes, ma'am."

"The entire standard set," Martin added.

Victoria looked at Martin, instantly realising what he meant.

"Sex drive definitely does not seem to be her motivator." Dr Elms leant against the desk. "Bet Director Morten would be pleased to hear that."

Victoria suddenly looked around. She checked her watch. Her team looked tired.

"Okay, Dr Elms, Anthony, Martin, you've done really well today. Why don't you call it a night? You've been at this for hours. I'll finish up here. We can tackle this again tomorrow."

"But Dr—" Dr Elms started to protest.

"I insist." Victoria was firm. "I cannot allow you to make any mistakes, least of all due to fatigue on account of being pushed too hard." Besides, she had an idea and she needed privacy to test out her hypothesis.

When they realised that she would not take no for an answer, Dr Elms, Anthony and Martin packed up swiftly and headed out the door.

Victoria noticed Jesse was not making a move from his usual place near the glass.

"You must be tired too," she said. "You can take a break too, if you want. I'll call you when I'm done."

Jesse shook his head. "No, ma'am. I'm good." Then he hesitated. "Unless you need me to leave?"

Victoria thought about it for a moment, then shook her head.

"Could you go see if she's okay to do one last session, please?" She hoped Sam would be okay for a little while longer.

Jesse nodded and without hesitation headed into the Lab.

Victoria had a theory and she really needed to test it, but she figured it would be best not to have the other three scientists present. As for Jesse. She liked him and felt she could trust him—well, at least she could trust him with having Sam's best interests at heart.

She once again studied the E.C.G. printouts. Dr Elms was right it did show a more or less flat graph. On closer inspection she noticed a slight spike near the section marked 765, for the 765th slide. She headed over to her computer and typed in the numbers 7, 6, 5, and hit the enter key. On the computer screen appeared an image of an androgynous boy. She scrolled through the rest of the Standard Deck of images. All the images were more or less stereotypical straight, girly girls and hunky men.

Victoria glanced at Sam and Jesse in the Lab. Could her instincts have been right? Could Sam be attracted to women? That day in the restroom she had felt something between them. But since then she had convinced herself that it was just her own weakness trying to see something that was not there, trying to read and interpret things as she wanted to see them.

If, however, Sam was not heterosexual and had deviant

sexual predilections, then it would make sense that the Standard Deck would not register an adequate response.

Victoria returned her attention to the computer. She selected "Search Type" and changed the selection from "Standard" to "All". In the search box she typed "androgynous, strong woman." The search rendered fifty-seven results. Not a lot, considering there are over twenty-thousand images in the Libidinal Analysis category. With the way the State was controlling everything, she reminded herself that she should be grateful she was allowed to retain the fifty-seven items in the interest of science.

She clicked and scrolled through the images. They included images of warriors, Amazons, women in business suits and women wearing men's clothing.

Victoria sat back and once again studied Sam through the glass. She needed this to be conclusive. Somehow she doubted a few women in business suits would prove enough of a stimulus for an irrefutable result.

She returned her attention to the computer and typed "lesbian, sapphic love." This time the search rendered thirty-nine results. She clicked and scrolled though to find images of women holding hands, kissing, embracing and being intimate. That should do, she thought. She clicked "Add".

Victoria got up and headed over to The Auditor where she flicked its small switch from "On" to "Off".

Returning to the desk in front of the one-way glass she pressed the intercom button. "Are we good, Mr Wyatte?" she asked.

The E.C.G. needle gave an excited little shiver, in the corner, unnoticed.

Jesse waited for the nod from Sam before he gave Victoria the thumbs up. "She says she's good." Jesse smiled.

"Okay, then, let's go," Victoria announced.

Victoria hit the "enter" button on the computer keyboard. Images started flashing up on the screen in the Lab, the newly added ones interspersed with a standard control sample. The E.C.G. needle registered an increase in activity at first intermittently until finally it went frantic. Victoria hit the pause button to halt and freeze the images that were being presented to Sam on the large monitor in front of her. She then went over to the E.C.G. printer. She waited a few seconds and then hit the pause button before ripping out the graph paper so she could take a closer look at the printout. The wavelengths were almost at full amplitude. She returned to the window to look at the monitor in the Lab to see which image could have caused such a strong response. There on the screen was an ultra-high definition image of two women, naked, making love, one with her head thrown back, her mouth open—the passion, desire and arousal clearly evident in their expressions.

Victoria flicked the intercom on. "Okay, Jesse. You can take her to get some rest. Thank you." After a brief hesitation she added, "You did good, Sam."

Once Sam and Jesse had left Victoria cross-referenced some of the earlier anomalies she had noticed in the test results with the new information to confirm her suspicion. Then she crumpled the recent printout into tight balls and lobbed them into the dustbin.

She restarted the E.C.G machine and finally headed over to The Auditor to turn it back on.

Jesse took Sam straight to her quarters. It had been a long day and even he looked exhausted to her. She hoped he would put her silence down to her own exhaustion. The truth is she could not speak for so many reasons. The day had been a complete sensory and emotional overload and sleep was the last thing on her mind.

Her brain was racing, looping through the activities of the day.

It all started with that innocent touch. Sam remembered the tingle she felt in her fingers as the Doc shook her hand when she came to introduce herself. She was sure the Doc felt it too. She must have. Their mutual attraction was palpable, even from that first moment in the restrooms.

Sam had meant to see if she was still wearing her ring or if she had lost it once more. She promised herself she would say something to the Doc about that the following day, as a little test or a reminder.

Then there was that curious expression on the Doc's face when she was injecting her. It felt like the Doc had felt the same pain.

The rest of the day had been pretty uneventful in terms of the tests she had to take. She was sad that the Doc did not come back into the Lab, but it felt good knowing she was there in the Observation room. She realised all her biorhythms were being monitored, so she had to use all her training to keep calm whenever she heard the Doc's voice over the intercom. Luckily she had been trained in how to cheat lie detection tests.

But, the thing that really had her wired was the last set.

In general the tests were pretty transparent and she could very easily identify what they were looking to ascertain. The only question that she still had to figure out was: To what end? That was until she was presented with the last set of images. She had certainly responded to them. She was also pretty sure that quite a few of those images must be illegal. She guessed that institutions such as this must be exempt from contraband legislation; however, she was sure, even then, some of those images must have required special dispensation.

At first she tried to trick the sensors, initially worried about what might happen if they discovered her true orientation. That resolution did not last long. From what she could tell the Lab had cleared out and it was only the Doc and Jesse left. She wondered what could have been the reason for that. It was with that knowledge though that she decided not to try to fool the sensors. Something in her wanted the Doc to know she was responding. All she could think about was that the Doc was on the other side of the one way glass watching her, knowing she was reacting. She wondered if the Doc was turned on by those images too, or perhaps, could she dare to dream, turned on by her? That thought in itself was providing extra fuel to her fire.

She had resolved to focus on calming down in the quiet darkness of her quarters and not to give the not-so-hidden infrared cameras the satisfaction of watching her take matters into her own hands.

After two hours of tossing and turning, and being unable to think of anything else, other than the Doc, she was about to give in to her need. She knew it would only take a few seconds before she came. She wondered where the Doc was now and if she could perhaps be touching herself too? Oh how exquisite that would be, Sam thought, visualising the Doc in the throes of an orgasm. But from what she knew about Dr Victoria Henderson, that was not likely. She had far too much self-control and would never allow herself such an unprofessional indulgence, especially not involving thoughts about a Subject.

With that Sam hopped out of bed and dropped to the floor to complete a number of rapid push ups and sit ups, in the hope of bringing on sleep through sheer physical exhaustion.

7

Jesse had been around for a couple of hours already. He had gotten Sam up, ready and settled her in the Lab with plenty of time to spare. The whole team had worked hard, again subjecting Sam to hours of image after image. Finally at about 11:45 Dr Henderson called a break and more or less ordered everyone to go to the canteen and have a cup of tea and something to eat.

Jesse had made Sam comfortable and then headed to the canteen to get them both a cup of tea and a bagel. He brought them back to the Lab because Sam was confined there while she was so heavily under the influence of the drugs needed for the testing. After she had eaten he returned to the Observation room.

When Jesse walked in, Dr Elms and Martin were busy setting up for the next part of the day. Dr Elms was particularly short tempered that morning. Jesse decided to continue to keep a low profile. He remembered about the Psych Eval Report that Dr Henderson had asked him to do.

Just then Anthony entered, eating a cream pastry. Even

he looked a little sullen. Jesse assumed the lack of progress was not good for their morale.

"I wouldn't bother with that. Nobody really looks at it." Anthony said in passing as he headed over to his desk.

Jesse ignored him and continued to write his report. Dr Henderson did not ask very much of him and he as sure as hell was not going to neglect his duties just because someone else in the team reckoned his job was not important.

Two seconds later Dr Henderson entered and saw him writing. She smiled at Jesse and nodded.

"Great, you are all back early. Thank you for that. We have a lot to get through," she said. Jesse noticed she, unlike Dr Elms, Martin and Anthony was not in possession of a hot drink. He made a note to self to ask her if she needed anything the next time he headed to the canteen to get Sam's refreshments.

"Have you checked the apparatus?" Dr Henderson asked Anthony.

"Just going to do that, ma'am," Anthony replied, stuffing the last of his pastry into his mouth.

"We haven't checked the sensors yet," Dr Elms said while he loaded the printers with more paper.

"Okay, I'll do that." Dr Henderson headed into the Lab.

Dr Elms had just switched the E.C.G. printer back on when the needle suddenly went crazy, startling him.

From his seat in the corner near the window Jesse watched Dr Henderson adjusting the electrode pads under Sam's top. Sam smiled and said something which Jesse could not make out as the intercom system had not been turned back on yet. Jesse noticed that whatever Sam had said caused a peculiar expression on Dr Henderson's face—a slightly awkward smile. He watched her remove her hands from beneath Sam's top and then vigorously rub them together before she continued to check the rest of the sensor pads.

Minutes later Dr Henderson returned to the Observation room.

"Jesse, I think you are the best at attaching those sensors," she said. "I think we'll insist you check them in future." She was laughing.

Jesse nodded feeling appreciative of her praise and a bit more validated as a member of the team.

"Is that better? Are we ready?" Dr Henderson asked Dr Elms.

"We just experienced some sort of surge," Dr Elms still looked puzzled.

Dr Henderson glanced at Anthony.

"Most probably due to picking up on your bio magnetic energy as well," Anthony suggested.

"There was one other earlier too, I noticed," Dr Elms said.

"I did make sure not to touch the sensors directly," Dr Henderson assured him. "What was she seeing earlier?"

Anthony checked the logs on the screen in front of him.

"A bear caught in a trap... Perhaps she's an animal lover?" Anthony said.

"Okay," Dr Henderson considered the information, "that could be emotive. Let's keep going and see if anything else gets flagged." After twenty minutes of images Dr Henderson peered at Dr Elms who shook his head.

"Still no movement," he said.

"Okay, let's move on to L.C.F. zero zero twenty-eight

next. Somewhere in there has to be a trigger we can use," she said.

Dr Henderson went to write in her notepad. She suddenly turned and started looking around, checking her lab-coat pockets.

"Anybody seen my pen?" She looked up and spotted it lying on the trolley next to the chair in the Lab. "Ah, there it is." She headed off to fetch it.

Once at the chair Sam looked up and gave her a broad smile. Jesse saw Dr Henderson smile back. Was he mistaken or was there real affection in that look?

Jesse's attention was drawn away from the Lab to the E.C.G. Printer which was suddenly going haywire again. Dr Elms noticed it too. He checked the camera feed from the Lab's internal cameras. Jesse could see Sam's smiling face on the monitor in front of Dr Elms.

"I don't understand this," Anthony broke the silence, clearly also flummoxed by the E.C.G. readings. "What does a Fork Lift and a hunted bear have in common?"

Just then a pager beeped. Jesse noticed Dr Elms retrieve his from his lab-coat pocket and read the message. Moments later he headed out of the Observation room without a word.

Dr Henderson returned soon afterwards. "What happened to Dr Elms?"

"I think he got paged, ma'am," Anthony replied.

She nodded and continued making her notes.

---

The following morning, around 09:00 there came a stern knock at the Observation Room door. Dr Henderson, Dr

Elms, Anthony and Martin looked around at each other, confirming that none of them were expecting visitors.

"Come in," Dr Henderson called.

The door swung open to reveal a slightly apologetic looking Director Morten followed by two armed Privates and a Corporal.

"Dr Henderson. Sorry to disturb you. I've been told this cannot wait," Director Morten said as he stepped aside to allow the Corporal and two Privates to step farther into the Observation room.

"Dr Martin Monroe?" the Corporal asked.

"Yes, that would be me." Martin looked up confused.

"You have to come with us." The Corporal nodded to his two Privates who stepped up to escort Martin out.

"Wait a minute. What's this about? This is my laboratory and Dr Monroe is one of my key staff. You can't just barge in here and take him away." Dr Henderson directed her incredulity at Director Morten. "Director Morten!?"

"I'm afraid I can't do anything, it's a matter of State," Director Morten said.

"At least tell me what is going on." Dr Henderson addressed the Corporal.

Martin seemed frozen in space, as if he had no comprehension of what was happening around him, while the two Privates cuffed him and started moving him toward the door.

Just then Jesse entered from the Lab where he had been giving Sam a drink of water and saw what was happening. His eyes met Martin's and he could see the terror, resignation and something else he could not identify immediately. Then, he realised that Martin must have been expecting and dreading that this day would come for a long time. That unidentifiable expression was one of relief – regardless of what happens now, he would have to wait in fear no more.

Even though he was not resisting in the slightest, the soldiers manhandled Martin toward the door.

"For God's sake, Hugo, what is going on? Stop them! Why are they taking him?" Victoria felt helpless and could not take it any more as she watched the soldiers disappear through the door with Martin.

Once the Corporal had also disappeared out the door Director Morten finally explained. "I believe Mr Monroe has been charged with breaking Directive thirty-seven—conduct related to homosexual activity."

"I don't care what he's been charged with. You can't allow this! He is one of my best Psych-Techs and an excellent scientist. I need him here!" Victoria's pulse was racing and her body tingling in outrage.

"Unfortunately, Victoria the State does not see it that way. There's nothing we can do." Director Morten said in a calm tone. He turned and also headed towards the door but stopped just before he reached it. "Dr Henderson, could we have a word." Then he headed out.

Victoria took a deep breath and followed him.

———————————

Outside Director Morten turned and addressed Victoria in a stern, verging on hysterical whisper. "Please can you make sure you screen your staff thoroughly in future!"

Victoria's jaw dropped. She was astounded by Morten's reaction, and the audacity of his accusation.

"We do not want this happening again. We can't afford unwanted attention," Morten continued undeterred. He was now pacing and rubbing his brow.

Victoria decided not to retaliate as she knew that would just make matters worse. Instead she glanced over and watched the soldiers march Martin farther down the corridor. She felt so helpless.

Morten followed her gaze.

"What will they do with him?" she asked softly.

When he did not answer she turned to meet his gaze, however he could not hold hers, and looked down at the floor before he turned and marched down the corridor in the opposite direction, leaving Victoria to her own thoughts. She could only imagine the horror that would face Martin now; being stripped of his identity, his mind reset to start a new life as a new asset to The State, a fate that would involve being released in to the world bereft of all memory of one's previous existence or previous loved ones.

## 8
———————

It was two weeks later. The team, what was left of it, had felt Martin's absence acutely each day. Sometimes Anthony would forget and address Martin only to be met by a poignant silence and an empathetic smile from Dr Henderson.

Jesse could not believe his friend had been taken. He had spent hours wondering what the Authorities would do to him and whether he would ever see him again. He had heard about this happening to others before and, according to all accounts, the person who got taken was as good as dead to their friends and family. Apparently, they would get taken to a top secret facility where they would be brain washed and reprogrammed, and then assigned back into society as blank individuals with new identities. In some cases, if deemed beneficial to the State, they would be allowed to retain the same set of skills and employed elsewhere in the service of the State. Jesse wondered how diverse Martin's field of expertise was and how well he was regarded amongst his peers. Was he respected enough to entice the authorities to allow him to keep his occupation? Even if that were to happen, how likely would it be that Jesse might bump into him again? This made Jesse very sad as he realised that even if that were to miraculously happen again, Martin would not be Martin.

---

The Chair in the Lab had been moved to one side. Sam was standing up in front of the bank of screens on the wall. Victoria wheeled over a large metal clad ring about half a meter in diameter on a flexi-arm stand. It reminded Sam of an antique photo her grandmother had shown her, when she was little, of her gran sitting in the hairdresser's with her head inside a large dome. Apparently that was used to dry hair without blowing it.

"The Simulation Ring picks up the alpha wave resonance from your brain," Dr Henderson said as she positioned the Ring horizontally about a foot above Sam's head like a halo.

Sam was finding it difficult to concentrate. This was the first time in days that she was allowed to stand freely, unhindered by the chair. The close proximity of Dr Henderson while she was setting up the Ring was completely distracting, not to mention the exquisite whiff of her delicate spicy perfume.

Sam had to literally bite down hard on her tongue to stay focussed on what Dr Henderson was saying. All she could think about was how exquisite it would be to lean in, to close the small distance between them and plant a kiss on the stunning doctor's very sexy mouth.

Sam suddenly realised what Dr Henderson had just said.

"Will it record all my unconscious thoughts?" A very uneasy feeling began to knot her stomach. What is this machine capable of revealing? It was one thing, subjecting herself to physical tests; it was quite another, revealing her deepest darkest desires. There are some things one does not want anyone else knowing, let alone the beautiful object of one's affection like this gorgeous woman in front of her. The implications were even bigger, as Sam so often had to remind herself. All the data and information about her would ultimately be at the disposal of the State. This could put her in grave danger!

Victoria understood why Sam would be nervous. She wanted to make sure that she explained the equipment and its limitations as fully as possible, to put Sam's fears to rest. For the experiment to work, Sam had to be relaxed and not worry about anything, least of all her privacy. Sam trusted her. She knew that.

"Yes, but general thoughts, both conscious and unconscious are unintelligible, just noise, not emotionally powered enough. That is what you will ultimately learn, to focus and empower a thought using your emotions. This is known as a Projection. You'll see it's not easy and requires considerable skill and practice, so it is very unlikely that non-deliberate projections will register on the Simulator." Dr Henderson pointed at the screen on the wall. "Also to protect your privacy this Simulation Ring has been calibrated to filter out signals below a certain level of intensity."

To make matters worse, Dr Henderson's cool fingers tickled and tantalised Sam's skin as she gently attached the sensor pads to her body, instantly sending little currents of arousal through her and causing her nipples to strain against the fabric of her top. Dr Henderson noticed her body's reaction and their eyes met briefly.

"Sorry, I'm almost done," Victoria said softly thinking that Sam's discomfort was due to her cold fingers.

"It is important that you understand that conscious thought is like a stop valve," Dr Henderson continued.

All Sam could think about was the tips of those cool fingers and she willed them to touch her, stroke her.

"It hinders the flow of alpha waves. So conventional conscious concentration is actually counterproductive; you've got to feel it, to want it—not will it."

Sam could hear her heart pounding in her ears. "So I've got to consciously make something unconscious?" she asked wondering whether this was a cruel joke. Did Dr Henderson know what effect she was having on her? She had to.

Luckily, just when Sam thought she could not take any more of this slow torture, Dr Henderson stepped away to switch on the Simulator Ring on the stand behind her. Instantly an amber strip lit up along the outside edge of the Ring. Dr Henderson went to switch on the screens on the wall in front of Sam and then turned back to check in with Sam one last time before they started. "Okay? You ready?"

Sam shrugged and smiled as best as she could. "You don't know until you try."

Dr Henderson took up her position next to Sam.

Sam closed her eyes and tried to focus.

"Now try formulating in your mind's eye a small, simple object such as a cube," Dr Henderson's voice was calm and encouraging.

Within a few seconds a brief monochrome orange

gaseous shimmer took shape on the screens, flickering in and out briefly before dissipating just as quickly.

Sam opened her eyes and let out the breath she was holding.

"Take a deep breath and let's try again," Dr Henderson encouraged.

Sam tried again. Her face became lined in a frown from the intense concentration. Once again only a brief orange shimmer appeared.

"Don't push it, Sam. Just let it come." Dr Henderson's voice was even and gentle.

Sam tried a third time. This time the gaseous form flickered and faded almost instantly.

---

Victoria could see Sam was getting despondent. She recognised how difficult it must be for someone like Sam, who was used to achieving, used to turning her hand to new skills without effort, to be faced with something she could not instantly conquer, and trying and failing while under scrutiny.

"Okay, okay. Stop. Stop!" Victoria tried to keep her tone firm but encouraging. She had to project confidence or Sam would lose it completely.

She walked around Sam, coming to stand right up behind her. She reached both arms round Sam's sides and placed her hands on her solar plexus. She felt Sam tense for a brief second. "It's okay," she reassured her.

"I don't think that is going to help," Sam croaked.

"Close your eyes." Victoria coaxed. "Now breathe in through your nose and out through your mouth."

Sam swallowed and then took a deep breath.

"Breathe into my hands. Focus just on your breathing." Victoria timed her instructions to the gentle rise and fall of Sam's solar plexus. "In… Out… That's right." She could feel Sam's frame starting to relax a bit. "Now, imagine a cube." She kept her voice low and soothing as she gave the instructions slowly, allowing Sam to act on each one while maintaining even breathing. "What does it look like? What can you see? In… Out… Feel its dimensions… its size. In… And out."

On the screens the orange vapours reappeared.

"Now… imagine touching it, running your fingers over the surfaces… one at a time. In… Out… It feels smooth… cool sides. The corners… pointy… joined by straight crisp edges. Feel the textures… the sensations. In… Out… Is there a smell? A sound? In… Out… Now… Covet it… Want it… Desire it."

A perfect orange cube took shape on the screens.

Victoria gently removed her hands from Sam's torso and stepped around slightly to the side and front of her, waiting for Sam to see what she had achieved.

Sam finally opened her eyes and, after a few moments of shocked awe, her face contorted into a broad grin. She was completely overcome with joy. In an unguarded moment she stepped forward and threw her arms around Victoria who was standing only a few feet in front of her. Instantly all the alarms and monitoring equipment burst into a cacophony in the Observation room. Luckily no-one was paying too much attention because everyone was too absorbed in their own elation and celebration. Jesse and Anthony spontaneously cheered and gave each other high fives. Even Dr Elms looked rather pleased.

Inside the Lab, the unplanned close contact between the two women grew thick with tension as they found themselves in a spontaneous embrace, inches apart, a split second away from kissing.

Just then, the Lab door flew open and Jesse, Anthony and Dr Elms came rushing in. The moment was broken and Victoria was yanked back to reality, like a bucket of cold water being thrown in the face, leaving her feeling acutely uncomfortable and awkward. She pushed Sam away making way for Jesse, who was rushing towards them to give Sam a victorious hug. Victoria turned away and started to gather up her notes on the trolley nearby, buying a few moments to compose herself.

When she turned back Sam was still enveloped in Jesse's arms. Their eyes met for a brief moment over Jesse's shoulder before Victoria turned and left the Lab.

What the hell happened there? Victoria chastised herself once alone inside the Observation room. How utterly unprofessional! She could not, and would not, allow Sam to get under her skin. Sam is a Subject! One does not go around hugging one's Subject or for that matter allowing a Subject to hug you. Slips like that could cost her her career. Not to mention that if the State got word of it, it could cost both of them their lives. They had seen what happened to Martin only a few days ago. She had to put a stop to this immediately! When she finally calmed down a little, she resolved to be extra vigilant. She needed to avoid all physical contact with Sam, to avoid time alone together, if at all possible, and to take necessary precautions, like remaining a safe distance away from her at all times, just in case Sam felt the need to lunge out in jubilation again.

———

It was around 18:30 hours. Anthony sat behind his computer and rested his head on the top of his pen, reinforcing the indentation in his forehead. He was struggling to stay awake due to exhaustion from all the early mornings and late nights that this programme demanded. On top of that all the waiting around was doing his head in. He liked his job because it was interesting, but during long experiments and exercises like this there was nothing to do other than monitor the instruments, the Auditor and the various printers, while waiting for Dr Henderson to finish with the Subject.

Jesse was waiting until he was required to take Sam back to her quarters. He was relaxed in his seat next to the one-way glass, feet up, absentmindedly observing the activity in the lab. Soon after Dr Henderson started personally overseeing Sam's exercises and experiments he realised that there would be very little need for his intervention. She was very hands on and attentive and Jesse grew to trust her implicitly. Even if her main object was to achieve the science, he was pretty sure she would never jeopardise Sam's well-being.

In the Lab the screens reflected six identical copies of a perfectly formed orange monochrome hard-backed chair. The gas dissipated and then just as smoothly reformed into the shape of an armchair, then a table, then a flex-arm desk lamp.

The door to the Observation room flung open, startling both Jesse and Anthony. Dr Elms stopped in the doorway, scanning the Lab and the activity in the Observation room. He had a blue file tucked under his arm.

"Progress?" Dr Elms more or less grunted in Anthony's direction. His sometimes curt manner was no longer a surprise to Jesse.

"This girl is a machine," Anthony said. "She seems even more driven than Dr H. I didn't think that was possible."

"Any noteworthy results?" Dr Elms asked.

"She has flown through the basic shapes. We're now onto simple complex structures."

"Okay. Good. In that case I'm going now. I have this," Dr Elms motioned to indicate the folder under his arm "to finish for the Director."

Anthony nodded and Dr Elms left as swiftly as he had appeared.

Jesse could see something was bothering Anthony but Jesse knew better than to ask questions. He knew Anthony would say something if he felt the need.

"It's okay for some." Anthony grumbled. "He can leave because he has a report to write."

Jesse listened and waited for Anthony to finish.

"I promised my wife I'd be home before the kids' bedtime at least once this week. It's been over four weeks since I've even seen little Ben."

Jesse thought about it for a moment.

"Well, why don't you go?" he finally asked.

Anthony looked up puzzled.

"I mean, I am sure I can finish up here."

Anthony still looked unsure but Jesse could see he was considering the offer.

"I know you Techs like to think your jobs are highly complex and beyond us mere mortals," Jesse continued, "but if you can do the truly complex stuff tomorrow, I certainly can watch the printers, collect the printouts and sort out the occasional paper jam, if needed."

Anthony pulled a face at Jesse's smart arse comment.

"I have to stay anyway and wait till they're done to take Sam back." Jesse sincerely felt for Anthony. He would have hated to have been the parent of a new baby boy and not be able to see him for weeks.

As it happened, Anthony did not need much more convincing.

"Great, man. I owe you one." Anthony packed up and was out the Observation room within seconds.

---

Sam looked exhausted as she once again failed an attempt to form an umbrella. "Nope. I can't get it."

"Okay, well you must be tired. It's been a long day. Let's continue tomorrow." Dr Henderson put down her notepad ready to pack up her papers.

"It's not rest I need," Sam complained. "It's these objects."

"What about them?" Dr Henderson said, distracted, as she had already shifted gears and was preparing to pack up and finish her reports.

"It's hard to feel anything about them," Sam said. "Come on doc, let me try something else."

Dr Henderson looked up and coolly assessed Sam, contemplating the benefit of giving Sam some slack. After all, she had really worked hard the past few days.

"Okay," she agreed hesitantly. "But last one. What do you want to do?" She expected Sam to suggest something more simple or familiar to her, perhaps. Being ex-military she expected something like a weapon perhaps or barracks.

In the Observation room, Jesse sat considering whether he could have a snooze. The very early mornings were catching up with him and he had not had a weekend off in about a month. That was his choice. He could not bear the idea of Sam being stuck in the Institute on her own.

Sam took a deep breath, closed her eyes and concentrated on her breathing purposefully.

On the screens the orange vapour reappeared as it had done countless times before. Slowly it took an oval shape. She had mastered the basic shapes quite easily. It seems they did not require much "motivation" as Dr Henderson called it. Progressively the oval morphed and started taking on more form and detail.

Dr Henderson finally put down the papers she had started gathering and turned her full attention to the bank of screens.

Slowly, the shape of a face, a head appeared. At first it was quite featureless, but moment by moment more and more detail appeared—the nose, lips, the eyes. Victoria held her breath, not believing her eyes. Soon a bank of six faces looked back at her from the screens, near perfect copies of… her face.

Sam opened her eyes. She studied the images and then smiled broadly, very pleased with her creation. "How's that?" She positively beamed at Dr Henderson.

Dr Henderson instinctively glanced at the one-way glass, her heart thumping in her ears. She grabbed her notebook and without saying a word marched out of the Lab.

"What?" Sam was completely thrown by Dr Henderson's reaction. "I thought you'd be pleased." She felt confused and devastated. What could she have possibly done to annoy her?

---

Dr Henderson stormed into the Observation room where Jesse was already up on his feet.

"Jesse, please take her to her quarters and see that she's settled."

Jesse rushed out into the Lab to get Sam.

Alone, Victoria stopped, looking out to see a bereft-looking Sam being freed from the numerous cables and electrodes. She sat down and collapsed her head in her hands. How could she not have seen that coming? That was entirely inappropriate. She should have stuck to her guns and not been so lenient with Sam. Now she had given her a noose to hang them both.

She glanced over at the monitor printer and saw the perfect printout of her own face staring back at her.

It would now be on record.

She reached over and ripped out the printout, crumpled it and stuffed it in her lab-coat pocket.

---

It was late. The rest of the institute had gone quiet with all the night staff and residents already asleep. Victoria sat in her office, tucked away in the almost deserted administration wing. She was practically the only person who occupied an office in this part of the building. She liked it that way.

Her office was a small, humble room. A plain wooden desk and chair stood almost in the middle of the room facing the door. She did not like the idea of having her back towards the door, and besides, she had to work on a lot of confidential documents, so it was prudent to prevent people from being able to peer over her shoulder easily when they came to see her.

The wall to her right, as she sat behind her desk, was lined with books. Against the wall behind her was a small couch which doubled as a bed when, on occasions like these, which were becoming ever more frequent, it was too late for her to drive home to her small flat in a nearby village. She had rented the flat specifically to make sure she had an excuse to escape the confines of work. However, Victoria could not at that moment remember when last she had been to her flat. Behind her, to the left, stood a large metal filing cabinet. She had to fight Morten to be allowed to bring it in as he wanted to keep everything high-tech and minimalist and could not understand the merit of storing hard copies anymore.

A small desk lamp cast a halo around her where she sat. She was struggling to focus on her paperwork. To the left of her against the wall a small fire crackled in the fireplace, a feeble attempt at driving back the emotional chill.

Eventually she stopped trying to read. She got up and went over to the fireplace, hoping its flames would thaw her tension along with the cold. She began to pace. Somehow, without even knowing it, she had headed down a rabbit hole that she was now struggling to get out of. How did this happen? Why did Sam have to become her Subject? Of all the possible outcomes. She did not believe in coincidences but these events were hard to explain otherwise.

As she pondered the day's events, she reached into her pocket where she felt the cool crumpled paper she had stuffed in there earlier. She pulled it out and smoothed it. Her own crumpled face looked back at her. She studied it for a while. The creases made her look older.

She really had no choice.

She crumpled and tossed the printout into the fire, watching her face contort as it was consumed by the flames.

## 9

Victoria had been up very early. Even though she was very tired she had not slept. She had checked her watch three times in the past five minutes. How she wished she could speed up time. Once she had made up her mind she hated waiting. It always made her tense.

Finally at 08:55 hours she could not wait any more. She headed to his office, even though she knew he didn't usually get in until 09:30 hours.

Director Morten's office, or rather his wing, was situated near the entrance to the institute, a position he personally chose when they first designed the layout. His reasoning was that he saw his role as a kind of "front man" for the organisation—the first port of call for the public, and hopefully the press.

The actual space consisted of a large, plushly decorated office and an equally spacious and luxurious reception area where he frequently made his guests wait for no other reason than to enhance the impression of his own importance.

This area was "manned" by Margery Duffy, a formidable

woman in her early fifties, a well-endowed mother of six who believed in using the same no-nonsense management skills and techniques in her day job as she used to control her brood at home. Privately, to close family and friends, she would happily admit with pride that Director Morten was like one of her children, number seven in the Duffy brood, and by far the most precocious one at that. To the rest of the organisation she was the self-appointed gatekeeper to Director Morten's office.

Victoria walked into the Reception where Margery was intensely focussed on a hard biscuit she was expertly dunking in her tea. She noticed that Morten's office door was closed which meant he was in.

"Morning. The Director in?" Victoria did not wait for a response.

"He's busy," Margery said not realising Victoria had no intention of waiting.

"Well this can't wait," Victoria said over her shoulder.

Margery, not knowing what else to do, stuffed the whole biscuit into her mouth before she bolted up from her chair and headed after Victoria.

In one smooth move Victoria knocked, opened the door and stepped into Morten's office.

---

Inside the office she found Morten, with a generous, somewhat leery smile on his face, perched on the end of his desk in front of two young female interns who were sitting upright attentively in the oversized armchairs in front of him.

"Oh, do come in, Dr Henderson." Morten got up and

buttoned his suit jacket as he returned to his chair behind the desk. "You are just in time. I was explaining the intricacies of PhyCorp's policies and procedures to our lovely new interns." He turned his attention back to the interns briefly. "Thank you ladies. That'll be all for now. If you have any questions Margery is also there to help you."

The two interns smiled coyly at him as they got up and headed for the door.

"Oh, and ladies, do remember I have an open door policy… so, if there is anything you need, just say," he added.

Victoria waited at the door for the interns to leave. Then she closed the door, shutting Margery out too, who had been hovering behind her trying to swallow down the dry biscuit so she could express her discontent at having been bypassed.

"To what do I owe this unusual pleasure?" Morten gestured to one of the luxurious armchairs, taking a seat behind his desk from where he brazenly appraised her physique as she advanced into his office.

She chose not to sit, hoping that this meeting would be swift.

Morten had known Victoria Henderson for over a decade and had made his interest in her known on numerous occasions. Each time she had artfully deflected his attentions, usually in the name of a professional working relationship. Even though he did not agree that a good working relationship and a sexual one necessarily needed to be mutually exclusive, he respected her enough to control his flirtations just enough to remain on the right side of professional—be it his definition of professional.

In reality, Victoria made him nervous. There was something so alluring, so enigmatic, and so utterly unpredictable about her, that he could not get a handle on her. That made him nervous, and he found it a complete turn on.

"Director, it's about the new Subject," Victoria said. "We need to turn her loose."

Morten was not entirely surprised by this declaration. "I've heard there have been a few irregularities, but what seems to be the problem?"

"Granted, her test scores showed incredible promise initially, however, we've been unable to identify a suitable trigger. We are simply wasting valuable time now," Victoria tried to sound as uninvested as possible. This was after all purely business.

Morten began to regret that he had taken a seat before she had. Having any woman look down on him, made him feel uncomfortable, like a naughty schoolboy before a headmistress—not an entirely unpleasant feeling but uncomfortable nonetheless.

"Please Dr Henderson. Have a seat," he said.

Victoria reluctantly complied and perched herself neatly on the end of one of the armchairs.

Deciding to turn the tables a little, Morten got up, and came to sit on the edge of his desk again as he had done earlier with the interns—a deliberate power move that enabled him to peer down at his new prey.

From there he could also enjoy a much better view of Victoria's more feminine assets, especially since she had not donned her regular lab-coat before coming to his office, perhaps on account of wanting to see him quite urgently.

He could not help marvelling at her smooth legs under the knee length skirt and the hint of a cleavage made visible by her silk blouse which elegantly, and just a little too modestly for his liking, covered what he imagined to be two small, pert breasts.

"I strongly advise, in the interest of saving valuable resources, that we regroup and focus our attention on finding other, more suitable, Subjects," she continued.

He was not always sure whether she deliberately ignored his advances or whether she was really so utterly absorbed in her work that she was genuinely oblivious to his attentions.

Morten considered her for a few more seconds.

"This is unlike you, Victoria, to throw in the towel so early?" He was not sure what, but he could see something was up and had clearly rattled her. He could see she looked tired and, judging by her clothing, he guessed she had probably not gone home again last night. Not that she was dishevelled or anything, just the fact she was wearing the same clothes she had on yesterday. He prided himself on being observant. That was one of his strengths, so he noticed things like that.

This was not entirely new behaviour on her part. He had observed her work on taxing, difficult projects before. He had even had similar conversations with her in his office, back in the early days when they had just started the institute. Back then all he had to do was play the confidence game and present as if there was never any inkling of doubt in his mind that they would succeed and somehow she would take strength from his bravado and leave his office, happy to go fight the big fight for them all. He was good like that, he knew it.

But this time... This time there was something more to

Victoria's visible discomfort. He could not place it and that bothered him.

"This is not about me," Victoria said. "I'm trying to put the interests of this organisation and this project first. We have successfully achieved the objectives of the pilot and proved that the science is at least possible, in theory. We now need to escalate the study with fresh Subjects."

Morten considered his response carefully.

"Victoria, don't get me wrong, I think you're doing a fantastic job. Without you this would be a mere dream." He paused allowing her to soak in his praise. "However, I don't think we could possibly have given her our best shot yet? This Subject could be the key to our, yours and my, success. Exactly what we've been dreaming of for this project. Who knows if there are others out there with similar aptitude? We owe it to everyone to persevere here. It's far too early to change horses."

"But Hugo, if we can't control or motivate her she is useless to us, and the project, regardless of her abilities. In the worst case scenario, if we can't control her, she could be a real danger to herself and others if we do happen to unleash latent abilities."

"Well, it strikes me that if you can't find a trigger... perhaps create one."

Victoria's face almost looked comical from shock, so much so Morten would have laughed if he was not in professional management mode.

"That would be extremely unethical, to manipulate a Subject like that, and I'm not even sure that it is possible, studies show—"

"Look, Victoria, you're a very gifted scientist—probably

the best ever in this field." When in doubt flattery was the most used weapon in his arsenal. Regardless of what people say everyone likes to be praised and that usually created a more receptive mindset. "I have full confidence that you can unlock this Subject."

Morten could see Victoria consider her options, more than likely evaluating whether arguing would make any difference. She was after all asking him not telling him.

"Okay," she finally said. "I will persevere, for now. But, Hugo, if we don't see notable progress in two weeks I'll be forced to submit my findings to the funding body."

And he scores. "Of course," he said with the required sobriety for the circumstances.

After only a moment's hesitation, Victoria got up and headed to the door.

Somehow needing to have the last word and priding himself on cultivating good morale amongst his staff he added, "Remember this is for the greater good and we are a team. So if there is anything you need, just come and ask."

Victoria briefly glanced back at him before she turned, opened the door and headed out leaving him feasting his eyes on her behind until she disappeared out of sight.

---

As soon as Victoria was out of view, Margery's head appeared at his door looking like she was about to launch into her usual tirade.

Morten held up his hand. "Not now Margery."

This stopped her in her tracks.

He picked up his phone and dialled a number.

"Please close the door for me, Margery," he said turning his back to her.

A few seconds later he heard the click of the door latch.

"I need you to do something for me," he said into the receiver. "I need everything you can get on Dr Victoria Henderson... Yes... All the way back."

---

In the Lab Jesse had just finished attaching Sam to the electrode sensors and was happily chatting to her when Dr Elms walked in.

Sam searched expectantly behind him. "Where is Dr H?"

"I will be conducting the session today," Dr Elms replied.

Her heart sank with disappointment. She had been eagerly awaiting the opportunity to see Dr Henderson after the previous evening's debacle. She had to talk to her to understand what she had done wrong and, for whatever reason, apologise. She did not mean any harm. She had meant it as a compliment and she genuinely thought that Dr Henderson would be pleased to see her true skills.

Dr Elms motioned to the one-way mirror and a harsh image of emaciated, badly tortured puppy appeared on the screen. Jesse who had retreated only a few feet from Sam visibly gagged at the sight. He immediately glanced toward Sam to see if she was okay.

The Lab door opened and Jesse and Sam instantly looked toward it, hoping to see Dr Henderson. Sadly it was Anthony bearing a file for Dr Elms.

"Orderly Wyatte, please tell the Subject to focus on the

images unless she wants her break privileges withheld today," Dr Elms barked at Jesse.

---

In Director Morten's office, Lady Frost, an elegant, only barely-tamed panther of a woman, was confidently draped in a chair. Her arms were relaxed on the armrests allowing Morten a full, unhindered view of her toned athletic figure. Her tight-fitting, blue suit accentuated her piercing cobalt eyes.

He was once again perched on the edge of his desk but looking far from in control of the interaction.

"Obviously Director, we were hoping for more. Judging by the intimacy of our relationship and the support we have extended… I, have extended… we expected you to fulfil your side of the agreement," she said.

Morten could not help it. She made him feel entirely intimidated all the time. Not even his most devious power tricks could give him any respite. There was something about Lady Frost that made his pulse race and his palm sweat. Every nerve in his body testified to the fact that she was deliciously dangerous, and he loved it.

"I can assure you, Lady Frost, that we are giving it our full attention and doing everything we, I personally, as well as the entire organisation, possibly can." If it was not absolute career suicide he would deliberately find things to slip up on to get her to come down there and tear strips off him like this.

"Glad to hear it," she said calmly with a smile on her lips that did not reach her eyes.

Those four little words caused waves of relief to course through his body along with all the other over active hormones.

He passively succumbed as Lady Frost got up from her chair and leaned seductively into him, taking hold of his chin with long, red-taloned fingers and kissed him deeply until he was breathless. Then she pulled away only a fraction, her red lips whispering millimetres from his ear. "If we do not have results soon then I will be forced to replace all the weak links... regardless of how close they are to me." As she uttered the word "close" she grabbed his crotch and squeezed none too gently. Then she leaned back into him and bit hard into his earlobe until she drew blood.

He could not help the small yelp that escaped his lips. As she withdrew he clutched at his ear.

She smiled that same smile at him, pushed away and made her way to the door.

He tried to compose himself as best as he could, retreating to the safety of his chair behind the desk.

Almost at the door she stopped. "Are we clear, Hugo?" she asked in a cordial, almost pleasant, tone.

"Crystal... As always, Lady Frost." He tried to smile what he hoped was reassuringly.

She sashayed out the door.

As soon as she was out of sight, he grabbed a tissue to tend to his bleeding ear.

Lady Frost always meant business. He nervously loosened his tie and jacket and cleared his throat in an effort to alleviate the suffocating feeling of fear that gripped him.

Later that evening Jesse took Sam back to her quarters. He wheeled her into the room. She was completely exhausted and had hardly said a word since they had left the Lab.

"Did you see her today?" Sam's voice was thin with fatigue.

"Who?" Jesse asked, at first not understanding what she meant.

"You know who, Dr H. Did you see her? Was she in the Obs Room?"

"No." Even Jesse had been hoping all day that Dr Henderson would come to the rescue. He was pretty sure she would put a stop to the harsh treatment Dr Elms was putting Sam through. After everything he had seen of her, he doubted she would condone such treatment of a Subject.

"I don't get it. Why is she avoiding me?" Sam said.

Jesse honestly felt for her. "I'm sure she's not avoiding you. She's probably just very busy. I'm sure she'll be back in tomorrow."

Sam looked at him as if to gauge if he was lying.

"Tomorrow. You'll see. Now you've got to get some sleep or you won't be in the lab tomorrow." Jesse put as much conviction behind his words as he could in an effort to reassure them both.

---

The following morning, the day began as normal. Jesse collected Sam from her breakfast and took her to the Lab. He helped her get set up for the day.

He could feel the nervous tension in her body as he fitted the electrodes. At even the slightest sound from outside Sam would glance at the door. He knew what she was thinking, hoping and boy was he hoping it too.

Finally the Lab door swung open and in walked Dr Elms.

Sam searched the space behind him. Sadly he was alone.

Sam caught Jesse's eye.

"Orderly Wyatte please finish up," Dr Elms said.

"Where is Dr Henderson? Why is she not here?" Sam asked, her voice quivering only slightly. "I'd like to speak with Dr Henderson." Sam was devastated but she gritted her teeth and raised her chin slightly in defiance.

"Dr Henderson has more important things to do today," Dr Elms announced coolly.

"I refuse to do any more tests until I get to speak to her." Sam's anger and frustration was beginning to crack her usually composed façade.

"Orderly Wyatte, please remind the Subject that the restraints are there to be used if the Subject is not able to comply with the requirements of the trials."

Sam and Jesse, both, were shocked. "You would not dare," Sam replied but both she and Jesse could see that it was not an idle threat and Dr Elms had every intention of following through with the incarceration if Sam did not comply.

Jesse realised he had to step in and save Sam from herself. "Sam. Calm down," he whispered.

"You said she'll be here," Sam hissed back.

"I don't know where she is. I'm sure she'll be back. But for now can we just stay calm and do as you've been asked." Jesse nodded encouragement.

"I need to see her."

Jesse's heart broke at the urgency and desperation in her voice. He had never seen her so vulnerable.

"I'll see what I can do, but please just do the tests." Jesse ran his hand across her forehead and over her hair in an attempt to sooth her. He had grown very fond of her and he really did not like seeing her so distressed.

Sam considered his earnest request, and the brief physical contact seemed to give her peace. She nodded.

Jesse looked up and nodded at Dr Elms who was busy consulting his notes. "She's ready to progress."

"Please fasten the restraints," Dr Elms said not bothering to look up.

"Dr Elms that won't be necessary," Jesse said. "She will comply willingly."

Dr Elms tore his eyes from his notes and looked at Jesse. "Orderly Wyatte, restrain the Subject for her safety, and ours," he ordered.

Jesse reluctantly tied Sam's arms and legs to the chair using the leather buckled straps on the leg and arm supports.

"It'll be okay," he tried to reassure a very spooked-looking Sam. "I'll be here."

"And her head, please." Dr Elms said as if in passing to Jesse and then directed his attention at the one-way glass, "Mr Phillips, please can you bring in the headset."

Jesse looked up at Dr Elms, surprised, but then saw Dr Elms was not even paying them any more attention. Very reluctantly he tied Sam's head, as gently as possible, into the head-restraint. He tried to keep eye contact with Sam, trying his best to reassure her that it would be okay. The problem was that he was not so sure.

Anthony appeared from within the Observation room

pushing a life-sized mannequin bust on a metal stand with wheels. The face of the mannequin was covered in a daunting oversized pair of electronic goggles, shaped with the intent to completely cover the eyes and ears of the wearer. It had thick cables extending out from the sides which were gigantic fibre-optic nerves bundled in fat plastic sheaths.

"Thank you Orderly Wyatte," Dr Elms' words yanked Jesse's attention away from the goggles. "Now please retire to the Observation room. I will call you if your assistance is required."

Jesse squeezed Sam's hand in a last attempt to convey strength and reassurance before he headed into the Observation room.

Dr Elms looked really proud as he took the goggles off the mannequin.

"Finally, it is complete. This is great day for science, Mr Phillips," Dr Elms said as he examined the goggles.

---

Anthony stood beside the mannequin, not knowing what else to do, feeling very uncertain and wishing he did not have to be part of Dr Elms' experiments. Unfortunately Dr Elms was his direct supervisor and he had very little say in what Dr Elms got him to do. Sometimes he had considered going directly to Dr Henderson for he was sure she would intervene if she knew about all of Elms' activities. However, that would seem disloyal to Dr Elms and although that did not bother him in the least, he was worried about what that would say to people he admired like Dr Henderson. Once you are seen as disloyal in the academic fraternity it would be very hard to find another mentor who would put their trust in you. And if Anthony was ever going to make Doctorate level and be able to properly support his growing little family he needed this job and he needed Dr Henderson's mentorship. Working with Dr Elms was, thus far, merely a technicality he had to sustain.

Dr Elms secured the goggles over Sam's face and head. He handed the plug to Anthony who plugged it in the nearby socket. Dr Elms flipped the switch which caused the fibre-optic cables to light up.

"Okay, Mr Phillips please get ready to record the results," Dr Elms said.

Anthony could not escape back into the Observation room fast enough.

Dr Elms adjusted a few dials and switches on the control panel attached to the middle of the stand.

"Now please focus on the images you see before you," he instructed Sam.

"Mr Phillips, please, press play," Dr Elms said in the direction of the one-way glass.

The fibre-optic cables started to flicker different colours and after a few minutes Sam began to whimper and shake, breaking out into a cold terrified sweat as she lay strapped in the chair, helplessly straining against her ties and at the complete mercy of the horrific images to which she was being subjected—all alone, caught in a terrifying world.

## 10

Director Morten strode down the corridor. He was not accustomed to patrolling the hallways of the facility, as he preferred to hold court in the client-facing comfort of his office. However, in order to run a successful enterprise one sometimes needed to get down on the shop-floor.

On this occasion he had a specific destination in mind. It would be his second visit in only a few days to this particular lab, but since there was so much riding on this project, he thought it wise to keep a close eye on it himself. When he reached the Lab he paused just outside the door, wanting to observe the interior activity first through the round vision-panel.

The Subject was lying supine, strapped down to the platform in the middle of the lab and connected to what resembled a rubber octopus smothering her face. Being a claustrophobia sufferer himself, Morten shuddered at the thought of having to endure such treatment, but he had taught himself a long time ago never to empathise with any of the Subjects. We all have to do what we have to do in the interest of State and the Civilised World. After all, nobody worried about him and what he had to suffer in order to make all this possible.

Finally, having seen enough, he pushed on into the lab.

"Director Morten!" Dr Elms nervously poked at his glasses looking a little like a startled hamster. "Morning. I did not expect you here, sir. If I knew you were coming I would have—"

"Dr Elms, is Dr Henderson around?" Morten glanced at the one-way glass wall.

"No Director," Dr Elms said, "I'm in charge of the programme for now."

Morten was a bit confounded by this but on one level he was not surprised. Victoria never did have the stomach for the hard stuff. "In that case can I have a word, please?" Morten retreated back into the corridor.

"Certainly, Director." Dr Elms made a note on his clipboard and downed tools. "Orderly Wyatte, please come and monitor the Subject until my return," he called through the one-way glass before he headed out after the Director.

Jesse did not hesitate. He rushed into the Lab, eager to see if Sam was doing all right. Dr Elms had had her attached to those goggles for three straight hours now and had refused Jesse's previous requests to allow her a break.

When Jesse reached her, with Anthony's help, he managed to remove the mask. He could see Sam was suffering a lot. He had no idea how to make her feel better so he settled for getting her a glass of water, feeding her cool sips and just letting her know he was nearby.

Through the round vision-panel, Jesse could see Director Morten and Dr Elms talking. Dr Elms was nodding profusely. Jesse could only guess at the content of that interaction. If there was a benevolent power in the universe it would result in stopping this barbaric treatment of Sam, however Jesse suspected that such a wish would never be fulfilled. When he saw Director Morten turn and head off, Jesse tried to think quickly. How could he possibly stall or get the exercises terminated for the day? Sadly he could not think quickly enough and without further ado he was dismissed to the Observation room and the experiments recommenced in earnest. He could not help noticing that there seemed to be an added vigour in Dr Elms' activities since his conversation with Director Morten.

It was well after 21:00 hours and Jesse was feeling decidedly uncomfortable about what they were doing. However, after everything Sam had been through that day, he did not have the heart to turn down her request. They were headed down the darkened corridor of the Administration Wing. He was acutely aware of every squeak emanating from the wheels of Sam's wheelchair. If they got caught it would mean the end of his career and he could not even imagine what it would mean for Sam. If it resulted in her being given a stern reprimand, severance pay and release from this programme, it could only be a good thing. He reconsidered. Knowing how valuable she must be to them now that she had demonstrated her potential, a fact that was clearly evident even though everyone was very careful not to voice it, he doubted a friendly handshake and well wishes would be on the agenda for her—more likely she would end up like

Martin. That, he could not bear thinking about. He
quickened his step.

"Do you know how much trouble we could be in over
this?" He looked around once more to make sure no one was
following them.

They approached a door halfway down the corridor, the
only source of light in the dark hallway apart from the knee-
high, blue night-lights that sat low on the walls.

"This is it," Jesse whispered as he parked the wheelchair
just outside the door. "You have fifteen minutes for whatever
the hell you need to say before I come in and drag you out."

"Thanks Jesse," Sam whispered, catching his hand briefly
in hers. "I owe you."

"You really do. I could get my arse sacked for doing this."
Jesse felt really touched by the small intimate gesture.

Sam squeezed his arm one final time before she got up
out of the wheelchair and stepped into the light.

———

Sam paused in the doorway.

Light classical music was coming from an indistinct
location inside the room. It was quite dark but as Sam had
spent the last fifteen minutes in near darkness with Jesse
making their way through the various twists and turns to get
to the Administration Wing, Sam could see quite clearly. The
main source of light came from a bright lamp on a small,
functional desk in the middle of the room. It was only once
she registered movement coming from behind the bright halo
cast on scattered paperwork that Sam realised Dr Henderson
was sitting on the far side of the desk.

Sam glanced around quickly and took in the furnishings. A set of open cabinets stood on the far side, behind the desk, against the wall. To the right there was a warm glow coming from the fireplace which cast a reddy-orange hue on the room. A 100cm by 100cm picture of Florence Nightingale hung on the wall above a plain dark couch which had a pillow and a blanket neatly folded on one armrest. Sam wondered how often Dr Henderson crashed on that sofa when she had worked far too many hours.

On the opposite side of the room the wall was clad with a wall-to-wall, floor-to-ceiling, bookshelf. There was a flicker of light emanating from the small crew lantern which was standing on one of the top shelves.

Sam took a deep breath and knocked on the door frame.

Dr Henderson looked up. Sam had anticipated the surprised look she got.

"Sam! What are you doing? You're not supposed to be here. How—"

Sam placed her finger to her own lips silencing Dr Henderson. "Please Dr Henderson, I really need to talk to you."

"Sam, this area is off limits." Dr Henderson reached out and picked up the phone.

Sam stepped into the office and closed the door gently behind her. She felt panic rise. She had to speak to Dr Henderson. "Why have you been avoiding me?" She launched in. She could not keep the emotion from stifling her voice.

Dr Henderson paused and then slowly replaced the receiver.

"You have not been in the lab in days," Sam continued,

not entirely sure how much time she had before Dr Henderson would change her mind and continue to make that call to security. "And even before that you hardly spoke to me—"

"I talked to you all the time," Victoria said.

"I don't mean giving me instructions or tests to perform. I mean like that day we met."

Victoria cleared her throat and reminded herself that she needed to handle the situation with utter professionalism. "Sam, you are a Subject now—"

"Yes, your Subject." Sam was not sure how to communicate everything she was feeling but she knew she only had this one brief chance to get it right. "The reason I became a Subject in the first place was you."

Victoria studied Sam as she considered the implications of this statement for a few brief moments. Sam looked rather frail standing there before her, unlike that first day they had met. In contrast, she looked radiant and almost invincible that day. The obvious distress Sam was in tugged at Victoria's heart. She swallowed down the urge to envelope Sam in her arms and tell her it would be all right. She could not afford to think like that, not about her Subject. She involuntarily propelled herself up out of her chair in an effort to escape those thoughts.

"Well, I'm really sorry to hear that." Victoria said evenly. "It was never my intention to mislead you." Determined to make that the last word on the matter she turned away to replace the folder in the open cabinet behind her.

Sam seized the moment.

Suddenly, Victoria became aware of Sam's presence right behind her; Sam's warm breath tickling on her neck. She froze and closed her eyes against the electrifying sensation as Sam pressed her lips gently to her shoulder and then her neck. Victoria battled shame and elation as she felt the acute ache as her nipples pebbled from the exquisite touch. Her will was not her own. She tilted her head allowing Sam more access. Her resolve crumbled.

Sam gently ran her fingers up over Victoria's arms, up and down her sides and then across her stomach, enjoying the taste of spicy perfume mixed with Victoria's natural scent as she nipped at an earlobe.

"It does not have to be that way," Sam whispered in her ear, hoping she could share the tremors that were running down her own spine.

Instead, it jolted Victoria back to sobriety. She grabbed Sam's hands, stopping them just before they reached her breasts, and she spun out of the embrace.

"I can't! This is not a game. My career, my life… our lives… are at stake. This is too dangerous!" Victoria felt as if she was fighting for her life. This was torture. She frantically sought refuge in the familiar armour of science. "What you think you're feeling is not real. It's infatuation… merely clinical transference."

"That is not true!" Sam would not believe otherwise. "I know what I feel. I know what I want… and I know you feel it too!"

"I do not," Victoria said evenly with icy determination.

Sam studied Victoria for a long moment, thrown by the calm, determined and detached tone with which she had just been rejected.

It took all of Victoria's resolve to calmly maintain eye contact, unflinching, until finally she could not hold it any longer and she turned back to the cabinet. "Now, please go back to your room or I will have to call security."

Sam's world shattered. The space around her warped instantly into that cold emotional desert she had found herself in so many times before, after she came back from The War. She felt utterly alone, dead in a living body.

She backed out the office quietly, closing the door behind her.

---

After a number of hours of tossing and turning in the dark, Sam had finally fallen into a deep, anxiety riddled sleep.

It was well after midnight when a shadow appeared under the closed door, cast by the low night-lights in the corridor.

The soft beeps of a pin-code being entered echoed along the silent corridor and then the door handle turned in the dark.

The door opened revealing the silhouette of a man in a lab-coat. He was pushing a trolley which had a small monitor and a portable Simulation Ring on it. He closed the door behind him quietly, and approached Sam's bed side. He waited listening to the soft sounds of Sam's breathing. Confident that she was still in a deep sleep he flipped on a small point-light on the side of his glasses.

It was Dr Elms.

He went to work quickly and quietly. He pulled the trolley closer to the bed and plugged the monitor into a socket on the instrument panel, on the wall, next to the bed. He then attached the Simulation Ring to the headboard and positioned it over Sam's head. Once he was satisfied the equipment was in place, he flipped three switches on the panel which caused the Simulation Ring's dim blue-black strip around the edge to light up and it to radiate a low electronic hum.

He reached over to the trolley and picked up a small syringe which had been carefully prepared for this purpose. He flicked the tip and then squirted a little of the luminous liquid out in the old fashioned style, before he carefully injected the small dose into Sam's arm.

Sam stirred slightly but did not wake.

He adjusted a few dials and flicked another switch. The monitor instantly flickered into life momentarily casting an unnatural white-blue hue into the darkness of the room. He watched the monitor for a few moments until the bright white-blue light was replaced with the usual dark screen. Satisfied, he finally turned and left as quietly as he had entered.

On the monitor in the dark a blue vapour took shape. It flickered and tried to take on form but collapsed in on itself just as quickly. This started a cycle of reforming and disappearing over and over again.

In the bed Sam became more and more restless. Her eyes flicked more frantically left and right as she dreamed.

## 11

Victoria had been working in her office since early morning. She did not have more than a couple hours of fitful sleep on her couch after the events of the previous evening. She felt ashamed at how her body had betrayed her and how she had let things get so out of hand with a Subject. She also deeply regretted having to be so heartless in her attempt to salvage the situation. Sam did not deserve to be treated cruelly. Victoria was the Doctor and was responsible for making sure that situations like this did not arise with her Subjects. She had worked successfully with hundreds of Subjects before without incident. Why was this one so different?

Her mind involuntarily flashed back to the feeling of Sam's lips on her neck, teeth slightly scraping over her skin. Instantly Victoria's body reacted once more. Goosebumps covered her skin. Her nipples bunched and a flutter spread down to her core... Oh God!

A light rap at the door ripped her back to the present. Director Morten stood in her doorway.

"They told me I'd find you here." He surveyed the office as if seeing it for the first time.

Dr Henderson jumped up from behind her desk. "Yes. I'm going over my notes and our findings to see if there is something we've missed. Dr Elms—"

"Ah yes!" he said with a little smile, "I won't keep you."

How long had he been standing there? Victoria tried to think what he could have seen. She tried to remember if she had actually let her hands wander over her body as she remembered the events of the previous evening. She was not sure.

Victoria tried to read Morten's expression.

"I just came to say I am glad you took my advice," Morten continued with a contented smile creeping across his lips. "Stroke of genius putting him on-point. Although his methods might not be to my taste, but perhaps tightening the reins is exactly what we need. Well done!"

For a few brief moments Victoria was caught off guard having no idea what he was talking about. Then she realised he must be referring to Dr Elms running through the rest of the stimuli tests for her while she did the preparation for the next set of exercises. But before she could reply and explain what was happening he had wished her a good day and was gone.

Victoria sat down staring at the now empty space where Morten had stood a few seconds before. What did he mean by "his methods?" Elms' methods? Why would he have commented on that? They should be pretty standard.

She got up and left her office.

Victoria approached the Lab. When she reached the door with its round vision-panel she stopped and observed the interior of the Lab.

At first she could not make sense of what she was seeing.

Sam was on the chair, but she seemed to be tied down with restraints. Her face was covered by some kind of mask headset which had thick bundles of wires extending out of it into a nearby monitor panel. There was something on her hands. Victoria could swear they were metal clamps around each finger conducting electrical currents from a nearby control panel.

Sam seemed fretful and was moving around, fighting and tugging at her restraints. If Victoria was not mistaken, she was exhibiting terror responses and seemed to be in an immense amount of distress and pain. Victoria could see Sam's body was covered in sweat. It was then that she glanced at her face again and noticed she had a rubber gag in her mouth. At this point Sam groaned and bit down hard as what seemed like a high voltage shock coursed through her body.

Victoria could not believe her eyes. How could this be happening?

She glanced around at the rest of the Lab. It was then that she noticed Jesse huddled in the corner, biting his fists, flinching at every shock.

At that point Victoria burst through the door.

"What the hell is going on here?" Though her blood was boiling, her voice carried a steely reserve.

Dr Elms looked up as if not understanding the question.

"We are in the middle of a conditioned-response

elicitation," he said plainly. "You know, to derive a trigger, ma'am."

"I know what conditioned-response elicitation is Dr Elms. Who is God's name asked you to do this?"

"Dr Henderson, you did," he answered. "You said to continue with the Trigger elicitation."

"Dr Elms, I said find a trigger, not torture the Subject!" Victoria's seething anger threatened to brim to the surface. She fought the urge to cause Dr Elms physical harm.

"Untie her immediately!" she instructed Jesse. "And make sure she gets a full medical check-up."

Jesse did not wait to be asked twice. Within seconds he was at Sam's side and had loosened her restraints and was helping her sit up.

Once Sam was free of the mask and the clamps, she glanced over at Dr Henderson. Their eyes met for a brief moment.

Victoria wanted to reach out to her, to apologise, to make it better. But how could she? It was best to keep her distance. After all, how could she expect Sam to forgive her after what she let happen in her Lab?

"Dr Elms, my office, now!" She turned and headed straight back out the Lab.

Never had Jesse been so pleased to see the back of someone as when Dr Elms downed tools and headed out after Dr Henderson.

———

The clock read 22:45. It had been a very long day.

After Sam refused the option to press the red button and

eject herself from the programme on account of those horrific events, Victoria had tried to insist that she at least took a few days off to recover. However, even that she refused and insisted she was fine to continue. There was nothing Victoria could do about it. She could not force Sam to drop out any more than she could contravene Morten's directive to keep going with this Subject.

Sam stood unrestrained, leaning, supported by the chair which was now in a standing configuration. The Simulation Ring was in position above her head. Once again her body and temples were peppered with sensors and electrode pads.

Dr Henderson was putting her through her paces, improving her skills at projecting images by harnessing her subconscious and channelling desire.

Sam closed her eyes and orange vapour appeared on the screens, then took the shape of a fountain complete with water spouting out of the top and a swan swimming around in the basin.

Sam opened her eyes and was very pleased with her efforts. However nothing pleased her more than the approving smile she received from Dr Henderson.

She was very relieved to find that after she had removed Dr Elms from the Lab and done whatever it was that they had to do in her office, Dr Henderson had returned to take full, hands-on control of the Lab activities. Since then Dr Henderson had been very gentle and kind, even slightly affectionate to Sam. Sam felt elated. It seemed her fear, that Dr Henderson would despise her after she had overstepped the boundaries in her office that night, was unfounded. Perhaps there was still hope!

"Okay. Very good." Dr Henderson gave her another

warm smile. "I think that's enough for today," she said as she switched off the screens and returned her attention to her file.

Sam pushed away from the chair but found herself quite constricted by the monitoring equipment, umpteen electrodes and cables attached to her.

Dr Henderson noticed and immediately stepped up in front of Sam. "Here let me get those for you." Dr Henderson reached up and began to remove some of the electrodes.

Sam lifted her arms out on either side to give Dr Henderson more access to her torso like she had become accustomed to do for Jesse.

"I never did say, thanks," Sam said.

Victoria looked a little confused. "For what?"

"For rescuing me," Sam said softly. She suddenly became aware of a building feeling in her chest and body that was threatening to explode out from behind her ribcage.

"I am sorry that happened," Victoria replied, genuinely remorseful and tender in her response.

She glanced up bringing her face to within a few inches of Sam's, who was looking down at her from the raised platform.

Their eyes met.

Sam noticed Dr Henderson's eyes dart instinctively down to her lips.

Sam's heart pounded in her chest.

It was now or never.

Still wired with electrodes, Sam reached her arm around Dr Henderson's neck and pulled her into a kiss.

At first it was just a tentative brushing of their lips. When Dr Henderson did not immediately pull away Sam deepened it and soon it grew into a passionate exploration of mouths and tongues.

Meanwhile, in the Observation room, the monitors, printers and instruments erupted in a cacophony of beeps and sirens as the system registered the sensory and synaptic overload.

Victoria felt completely engulfed in an erotic haze. She wanted to succumb to it, to let go and allow herself to fall into it.

Somewhere in the recesses of her mind she registered a voice telling her—no screaming—for her to stop, but she could not. She wanted more, much more, deeper, rougher, to be possessed and to possess.

Around them the lights flickered, alarms sounded and sparks dropped and fuzzed to the floor as the electronic equipment began to overload. Finally the lights surged and, with an extra fizz and a pop, the main circuit-breaker blew leaving them in the dark-blue glow of the emergency lights.

"Attention. System overload. Attention. System overload," the electronic voice of the security system echoed through the room.

This dragged Victoria back to her senses and to what was going on around them. She finally managed to pull back, breathless.

"Christ!" She tried to clear her head. "That was either the kiss of death for both of us or you have about," she checked her watch, "thirty-two seconds to think of paint drying to calm your bios."

Victoria grabbed her clipboard and rushed out of the Lab.

A few long minutes later the security alarm finally stopped and the Lab lights restored.

Sam started to remove some more electrodes, but in a flash Jesse appeared by her side and took over the expert task of setting her free.

All the way back to her quarters, Sam felt elated. Her lips still tingled from the passionate kiss. She could not remove the smile from her face even if she wanted to.

Jesse on the other hand was uncharacteristically quiet.

"They'll fetch you at seven-thirty for breakfast," Jesse said plainly as he engaged the wheelchair brakes.

It suddenly struck Sam that Jesse had not said anything since he returned to the Lab after the lights fused. Sam's smile faded. There was definitely something up with Jesse. He always fetched her for breakfast even though he did not have to. She knew he usually prided himself in being her number one carer and providing almost all of her care if he could.

"What's eating you?" she asked.

"Nothing," he responded without looking at her.

"Can't be nothing," Sam said as she got out of the wheelchair. "You've not said a word since we left the Lab. Not even chewing my ear off over how I should drink more water or take more breaks."

She studied him waiting for a response and saw him visibly capitulate. She wondered whether he knew he gave all his thoughts and feelings away on his face.

"You really want to know?" Jesse asked. His voice had an unfamiliar tone to it.

"Yeah, I wouldn't ask otherwise."

"Okay, I'll give you what you want, since that is all that matters to you it seems. Right?"

"What are you talking about?" This was the last sort of response she expected from him.

"You want to know what's up?" He paused briefly an agitated tongue darting out to wet his dry lips. "You. That's what. I had not realised how utterly self-absorbed and selfish you are."

"What—"

"No! Shut up! You wanted to know so, for once, you'll listen."

Sam decided it was best not to interrupt but allow him to get whatever it was off his chest first. She sat down on the bed waiting and listening.

"At first I didn't get you," he said. "I didn't understand why you would volunteer for a programme like this, with such high stakes and so much to lose. I admired you, thought you were a hero, a person with integrity, a far better person than I could ever be—doing this for the greater good." Jesse shook his head. "How wrong was I?" He began to pace back and forth.

Sam dropped her head, setting her jaw, waiting for the tirade to finish.

"What really floored me was when I saw how much you supposedly care for Dr H and even seemed to care about me, but yet, you deliberately set out to endanger us all. Sam, I don't know what demons you're fleeing from, or why you would have a death wish, but why would you take her down with you?"

"I'm not taking anyone down—"

"You will push, and push, and push too far," he said. "Well, I'm not going to stick about and watch how you hang yourself and take us all with you."

Sam had had enough. She got up and confronted him directly. "Jesse, I learnt a long time ago, people make their own choices." Sam noticed Jesse flinch away from her. "You can only take responsibility for yourself," she said in a more reserved tone.

"Okay," Jesse said, looking relieved when he realised that she was not going to lash out at him after all. "Well, in that case, it is time I do that."

"Do what?" Sam said. "What do you mean?"

"I mean," his voice was calm with a certain finality to it. "I'm stepping down as your P.C.A."

Sam suddenly felt panic rise within her at the thought of losing her only friend. "But Jess—"

For Jesse the conversation was over, he turned and left, closing the door behind him, and locking it.

## 12

Director Morten sat in his office reading the incident report. It was exceedingly thorough, which was very much like Dr Henderson, but he still felt uneasy about it. Why in her Lab? Why while she was working with the Subject? What exactly could have caused such a large drain, and then a surge big enough to cause the circuits in a multibillion pound lab to fry? The entire research facility was excavated out of solid rock on the Cornish Coast so he could believe that the infrastructure would be temperamental, nevertheless—

A commotion in the reception area of his office interrupted his thoughts.

"Margery?" he called out irritated. "What seems to be the matter?" He removed his reading glasses while waiting for a response.

Margery appeared at the door looking rather apologetic and frazzled with her fingers tightly locked across her solar plexus accentuating her rather well-endowed bosoms. "Director, it is Dr Elms. He seems to have something for you, sir, which he insists on delivering in person."

Morten considered the options. The incident report could wait for the moment, until he decided how to deal with it.

"Very well," he said waving his hand. "Let him in." Honestly! Sometimes Hugo Morten felt like a referee in a playground skirmish.

A triumphant looking Dr Elms appeared behind Margery and pushed past her into Morten's office.

Margery, nose in the air, in a visible huff, disappeared back to her desk.

"Director, I have the recording you asked for," Dr Elms said. He retrieved a small silver USB stick from his briefcase and held it out as if it was a precious heirloom. "I think you'll find the contents... interesting."

Morten peered at Dr Elms. "Very good, Dr Elms." He gestured for Dr Elms to put the USB stick down on the table. "Thank you." Morten replaced his reading glasses on his nose and returned his attention to the report.

A rather dejected looking Dr Elms placed the USB stick down gently on the desk. He turned and headed to the office door. Here he briefly hesitated as if he was about to say something but he thought better of it and left.

———

Later, Morten was in the middle of doing his weekly report for the Board when Margery knocked at his door.

Morten looked up irritated. Did everyone have to take his 'open door' policy literally?

"This just arrived as a special delivery for you, Director," she said, holding up a thin document sized parcel.

He nodded toward the end of his desk.

She smiled her best smile and approached, bending down lower than needed to show extra cleavage as she lay the parcel on the edge of the desk.

He did not notice her. He stared at the parcel for a long moment unconsciously licking his lips, his mouth suddenly dry. "Close the door please." His voice was distracted. "I do not want to be disturbed." He was no longer aware of anything else around him other than the countless potential the parcel could contain.

Margery left feeling under-appreciated for the second time that day.

Margery sat at her desk engrossed in an underground gossip magazine—her essential reading equivalent to what the Telegraph or the F.T. would be to a business person. There were not many such magazines around these days since most of the news revolved around the war and the State. As a result she savoured every article rereading each one a few times. This one was particularly juicy, complete with photographs, about another celebrity, a gorgeous male film star who was outed as batting for the other side and dragged off for Reset. The worst part of it was that he was married to another T.V. star with whom he had had three children. The article claimed that their marriage was yet another celebrity marriage of convenience to hide their true affliction.

When the intercom buzzed she pressed the button to answer it without taking her eyes off the page. "Yes, Director," she said putting on her accommodating voice.

"Get me Dr Henderson, immediately, please."

Director Morten sounded stressed. That got her attention.

"Certainly Director."

---

Director Morten sat behind his desk, elbows resting on his chair, staring off into the middle distance to one side of the room.

Victoria walked in agitated at being called away from her research. "What is this about, Director?" She needed to get this dealt with as soon as possible and get back to work.

"Come in and close the door, please," Director Morten said.

Victoria could see something was definitely up with him. His demeanour was different, troubled. This threw her a little. She did as asked and approached his desk but remained standing in front of it.

From her position she could see he had the Incident Report open on his desk. Her heart started beating faster. She was sure she had crafted that report impeccably. It was not difficult to explain away an incident with the electrics to someone like Morten who prided himself on keeping sight of the big picture. Had she made a mistake and given herself away. She tried to think back to what she had written.

"Please have a seat." His voice was calm, too calm.

"We are in the middle of the drug trials on the primates. I'm really keen to get back to the Lab to make some progress—"

"And have you?" he said.

"Have I what?"

"Made any progress?"

"Nothing significant, as yet," Victoria admitted cautiously. "I can't help it that this Subject is just not responsive."

"Oh? I believe, by all accounts, she is very responsive."

Victoria was puzzled. Where was this going?

"Please sit." Morten said again as he leaned over and picked up a remote control from his desk and pointed it to the large wall mounted flat screen.

Victoria took a seat.

The flat screen blipped into life revealing pulsing, monochrome blue vapours.

"What is this?" Victoria asked. She finally took a seat not knowing how long this pointless spectacle was going to take.

Morten ignored her question and fast forwarded a little and then pressed the play button on the remote.

The vaporous shapes slowly pulsated on the screen for a few agonising slow seconds before it began to coagulate and took on a more solid form, two forms, two perfect heads. Then the forms grew animated and Victoria watched in horror while deathly silence turned into a raucous ringing in her ears. How could this be possible?

"Where did you get this?" Victoria asked unable to keep the shock out of her voice.

Morten let the recording loop a few times in slow motion before he finally hit the pause button freezing the frame on an image of Sam and Victoria in a passionate embrace, kissing.

Victoria did not know what to say. Her mind was momentarily foggy from the shock and the repeated question of where the recording could possibly have come from.

"Although I'm not a scientist, it struck me, if one is looking for this illusive subconscious trigger then dreams are probably a good place to explore—a hunch that Dr Elms confirmed and then actioned for me," Morten said.

"We do not farm dream sequences! Unconscious desires do not tend to be clear and coherent enough—"

"That looks pretty clear, don't you think?" he said.

Victoria finally broke through the fog in her mind. "Director, as you know, Subjects often fixate during the trials. It is ephemeral and not reliable as a trigger... This is unethical and an invasion of the Subject's privacy!"

"Hers or yours?"

"I beg your pardon?"

Morten reached over and grabbed a file which was lying closed on the desk next to him that Victoria had not noticed until then. He tossed the file casually, allowing it to slide and come to rest on the table in front of her.

Victoria had a really bad feeling about this. "What's this?" She picked up the file and opened it.

Her brow began to tingle as she studied the contents of the file—images and memories of long forgotten sins, youthful transgressions she had firmly put behind her, flooded her senses.

"Where did you get these?" she asked trying to control the rising panic that gripped her throat.

"Never mind where I got them. The fact that they exist in the first place, is what should concern you."

Victoria flipped through the images to find a fifteen page, typed report.

"It makes for an interesting read," Morten said. "And one I'm sure the Board, and of course the State, would find fascinating." Morten emphasised his esses. Not unlike spitting venom; like the snake he is, Victoria thought.

"However, in the interest of time I'll summarise." Morten said with a matter of fact tone, getting up and rounding his desk to perch in his usual position on its edge towering over her. His demeanour was calm, almost friendly, as if he was preparing to relate a fairy-tale.

"It seems your 'gifted potential' had made you a 'subject of interest' much earlier than you might have suspected— right back when you were still a young 'innocent' undergrad, I believe 'struggling with your sexual identity'?" He was obviously thoroughly enjoying the theatrics of his speech. He got up and stalked around the back of Victoria's chair.

"Lucky for you this was a while before such," he searched for the word, "'extracurricular activities' became sectionable."

Victoria had heard enough. She got up and slammed the file onto the desk in front of her. "You have no right!" she seethed.

Morten lunged, his demeanour suddenly aggressive as he pushed up right behind her trapping her between the desk and his body.

"Oh but I do." His voice was a low, sinister whisper.

After a brief pause, seemingly back in control, he sensually tucked a stray strand of her hair behind her ear, inhaling her scent deeply through flared nostrils, before he retreated and continued his narration while pacing around the chair.

"It says there that being a budding scientist you decided to conduct a little experiment of your own." Morten chuckled to himself. "Why does that not surprise me?" He paused and looked Victoria up and down. "Did you think your little experiment could put this matter to bed, so to speak, once and for all? Or was that just an excuse to have your way with a dozen or so prostitutes, I wonder?"

Once again he came to stand tucked in close behind Victoria and spoke softly in her ear.

"Did they have to fill out a customer satisfaction questionnaire for you, after you," he grabbed her hips and thrust his pelvis forward into her, "fucked them?" Unbidden tears began to roll down Victoria's cheeks as she braced herself. His strong grip grabbed her upper arms and spun her round to face him, his pelvis pressed into her.

"Or did they fuck you?" he practically spat at her.

Victoria locked eyes with Morten, refusing to show her vulnerability, daring him to push this further.

He silently challenged her to fight back.

Finally Morten backed off.

Victoria soundlessly whimpered with relief as she swiftly wiped the tears from her eyes and forced herself to regain her composure.

"I have every right, Victoria." Morten continued. "I have worked my entire life to get to where I am and the holier-than-thou ethical considerations of some frigid dyke is not going to ruin it for me now." He took a few deep breaths to calm down. "I'm a practical man, Victoria. If you had just done what I'd asked it wouldn't have come to this." He paused to allow his words to sink in. "But now, I have no choice… unless…" he watched to see if she had guessed what he was going to say. He could see she knew where he was going to go with this so he nodded. "Yes…unless… you come up with some 'significant' results soon."

Morten let the implications of his words hang between them for a few moments before he returned to his seat, behind his desk, thereby ending the conversation.

Victoria felt too shaky and on the verge of tears to risk saying anything. She straightened up, set her jaw and headed for the door.

"Oh, and by the way I found out what happened to Martin." He added just before she opened the door. "He's now in an asylum, shitting in his diaper and eating through a straw. I think the term they used was a 'blank slate', ready to be reprogrammed."

Victoria paused for a brief moment, without turning back. Then she turned the door knob and headed out of his office.

## 13

Today would be their first time in what was supposed to be the new, state of the art, purpose built lab which she specifically designed for the third phase of the ADV Program. Unfortunately, the construction of the lab was about six weeks from completion and a mere skeleton of what it was intended to be. In fact, the team affectionately called it "The Cage" due to its bare, basic appearance.

Victoria's intention had not been to skip so far ahead of schedule, but due to the recent developments with Morten, she was forced to move things forward, a lot further than she was entirely comfortable with. Half the safety and backup systems had only just come online in the past forty-eight hours and that was only thanks to Anthony's hard work and brilliance.

Victoria had been resolute on doing certain aspects of this so early. She was adamant that, if Morten insisted on this foolhardy haste, as much risk and complication as possible needed to be removed from the situation. She insisted that the thirty-strong team of specialists that would usually be in attendance in the Observation room was reduced to herself and her core team only. And then only she and the Subject were to be present in The Cage during the exercises. She was not about to risk the lives of so many of the country's finest scientists. Thankfully, after Victoria pointed out to him the public relations nightmare that would follow any incident which put the lives of such a high-profile team at risk, Morten finally saw reason.

Additionally, it would be her responsibility to co-ordinate them all. Victoria was well aware of the merits and advantages of having a large, strong, specialised team; however, as their leader, one had to be that much more prepared. To be able to think ahead of them all you had to more or less know exactly what to expect at every turn. Right now, although she had worked twenty hour days for the past three weeks attempting to prepare for today, she still had no idea what to expect. She did not know whether the experiment would even work in the first place, let alone what the consequences or clinical results would be. They were attempting to postulate about possibilities of human potential so far off the known scale they might as well be dealing with aliens.

Another, unfamiliar orderly, had collected Sam again earlier for her morning routine of ablutions, gym and breakfast. During the last few weeks this had been altered somewhat. Victoria had explained to her that it was important for her to look after herself, by eating well, sleeping well and doing exercise to keep her strength up for the gruelling programme ahead. Apparently the next phase was going to be a steep change in the programme and they needed her in tip-top condition for that. Sam did not mind. In fact, she quite enjoyed being able to incorporate some physical activity into her daily routine and she certainly did not mind the improvement in the food she was given.

Now the same orderly, an older man with white grey hair wheeled Sam down the corridors to what she assumed must be the new Lab. She did not know much about it except that Victoria had warned her that they would be conducting today's lab work in a different location. Now that Jesse was gone, and no longer keeping her informed, Sam had little to console herself, knowing practically nothing about the actual information behind the scenes. In fact, on a day to day basis, she knew very little of her progress or even whether she did well in the tests or not.

It still felt really odd not to have Jesse around. She missed his familiar smiling face and the stupid jokes he told to try to cheer her up after a hard day. It was only now that she had to endure virtually complete strangers taking her through her morning routine that she really appreciated how fond she had become of Jesse. She wished he'd reconsider his decision and come back, but it was his choice ultimately. She had to confess that he probably would not have volunteered for P.C.A. on this programme, with its long hours and hard work, if it had not been for her talking him into it. She hoped that wherever he was now or whatever he ended up doing he was happy, enjoying his work, doing what he really wanted to do, and living the balanced life he deserved. She was almost certain he would probably be looking after some other unfortunate soul who needed his help. He was like that —kind.

As they passed through a set of dark-green, swinging double-doors at the end of the corridor, they entered a huge hall. Sam was awestruck by its sheer volume. It must have been at least three or four storeys high and felt more like a hangar than an underground lab.

In the middle of the hangar was a rectangular structure that resembled a metal enclosure. She instantly understood why the orderly had referred to it as The Cage.

Sam was relieved to see Dr Henderson already working in there. She was still not entirely confident that, after their last debacle in the Lab, Victoria might not still choose to have Dr Elms conduct the experiments with her. Without Jesse to intervene, there was no telling what extent Dr Elms would go to, given another opportunity.

When she kissed Victoria, the potential ramifications of her actions were the furthest thing from her mind. In that moment, even if she knew what she would have had to endure at Dr Elms' hand, it would have been worth it. In fact any consequences would have been worth it. Sam smiled to herself as she touched her fingers gently to her own mouth. Her lips still tingled at the thought of that kiss. What was even more amazing was that Victoria did not just allow her to kiss her but she kissed back! She was right. The Doc did have feelings for her.

The orderly brought the wheelchair to a stop just past the gap that was the gate in The Cage's perimeter fence.

"Thanks, James. That'll be all." Dr Henderson dismissed the orderly with a nod.

"Sam, if you'd like to take your place, please." Dr Henderson said pointing to one side of The Cage.

It was only then that Sam noticed the familiar Chair from the other lab standing to one side. Here, in this cavernous surrounding it looked small and almost insipid, as if it could hardly restrain a foal. The Chair had been reconfigured in a slanted, supported standing position.

Sam got up out of the wheelchair and walked over to The Chair.

From her new position she scanned the inside of The Cage. Like the original lab the back wall was made up of instrument panels and compartments filled with medical and scientific instruments and kit. In front of that was a large hip-high wooden workbench. On the workbench stood a large labyrinth of glass tubes that twisted and turned between containers, condensers and retort stands. It resembled a large, quite beautiful, glass sculpture due to the luminous green liquid bubbling through it.

Except for the gap in the cage perimeter that was the doorway, to her right, two of the three sides were covered in large heavy drapes. Sam was a little surprised by how rudimentary the furnishings were compared to what she had experienced in the rest of the facility, but then she guessed that they probably did not really need much for what they were trying to do.

Behind her, as in all the other labs, was a large one-way mirror, the usual tell-tale sign of the presence of an Observation room, built on to one end of The Cage. She briefly wondered whether Jesse might be in there looking out at her—a thought she rapidly dismissed. He was probably

long gone, either reassigned to the Day programme or
perhaps even working for another organisation by now.

---

"Today we are going to introduce you to a highly
sophisticated drug," Dr Henderson said pointing at the glass
contraption on the workbench. "What it will do, we hope, is
amplify your ability to the point where you can manifest
your projections in the real world."

"We hope?" Sam tried to smile. She was conscious of the
nervous butterflies fluttering in her stomach. Jesse would
always make her feel calm at a time like this. Now it was just
up to her.

Dr Henderson purposefully approached the chair. "The
drug is highly volatile and, with enough kinetic energy and
heat, is likely to combust. So, for your own safety I need to
strap you in."

"Bet you've been looking forward to tying me up for
ages, Doc," Sam said with a wink and a cheeky grin, trying to
deflect thoughts of impending doom.

To Sam's disappointment Dr Henderson did not respond
to the flirtation.

She did notice Dr Henderson's brief glance down at her
cleavage.

"Please can you take off any jewellery," Dr Henderson
asked. "It will be returned after we're done."

Sam realised Dr Henderson was referring to the
Lighthouse pendant resting on her chest. She lifted the chain
over her head and held it out, then paused. "Take, it. Keep it.
It's a gift," she said before she lowered it into Dr Henderson's

outstretched palm and curled Dr Henderson's fingers around it gently.

Dr Henderson took the pendant and dropped it safely into her lab-coat pocket before she proceeded to tie the buckles and straps around Sam's legs. As Dr Henderson tied her wrists in place, Sam reached out and brushed her fingertips across Dr Henderson's smooth forearm just above the wrist. Dr Henderson did not stop the soft caress but raised a reprimanding eyebrow.

"That glass chamber is a tank of highly charged nanoparticles." Dr Henderson pointed at a large empty glass chamber on a stand a few meters in front of Sam. "Think of it as one of the screens on the wall in the Lab before—a focal point on which to project your manifestations."

Dr Henderson headed to the workbench where she retrieved a small glass vial containing a luminous yellow-green liquid—a slightly darker and more concentrated form of the liquid bubbling in the glass tubes. On the way back she gathered up a syringe dispenser from a nearby trolley.

Sam watched as Dr Henderson loaded the vial into the dispenser.

"This will boost your receptors and heighten your sensitivity to stimuli." Dr Henderson gently sterilised the crook of Sam's arm with a small white swab. She then carefully positioned the needle end of the dispenser aiming for one of Sam's nice, big blue veins. As she shot the drug directly into Sam's vein the dispenser let off a quick high pressure hiss as it discharged.

Sam grunted and clenched her jaw at the sharp pain. "Oh, great!"

"Not only will it increase the pain inflicted but I will feel everything you do to me even more intensely?" She tried to block out the sharp burning sensation that was rapidly spreading up her arm.

"Yes, you will experience all sensory and... imaginary stimuli much more acutely. This is unfortunately a by-product of the desired effect of the drug. So you need to try to stay in control. If you feel your control slipping, follow the protocol. Immediately engage your breathing exercises and focus as you've been taught." Dr Henderson's tone was firm but Sam could detect something else. She was not sure what. Some kind of resignation, perhaps?

Suddenly, while Dr Henderson spoke, Sam's perception started to change.

The sounds around her warped, grew louder, while Dr Henderson's words seemed to become muted like they were drowning, being muffled by other sounds which Sam had not noticed until then. She tried hard to focus all her attention on Dr Henderson's lips. It was important to hear what she was saying. Those lips, those words were her only anchor to reality—to safety.

Bright sparks, like psychedelic fireworks, began to colour her vision. The blood started to thump extra loudly in her ears. Soon her entire body felt wired. Every nerve cell felt swollen and blooming, open, receptive to such an extent that even the slightest pressure of the air on her skin felt painful.

Her attention was arrested by the small area of skin where Dr Henderson's hand was still casually resting on her arm while she spoke. It felt like her skin glowed red hot under Dr Henderson's touch. The agonising ache grew into another excruciating fiery trail that ran up her arm—a scorching heat haze of desire as it swept a line to her chest and down to her core. Without warning her body arched as if an electric current coursed through it causing her to strain against her bindings. She expelled a low primal cry from the painfully pleasurable agony.

It felt like time had slowed right down. She could see Dr Henderson, leaning closer and talking as if in slow, distorted motion.

"Sam... Breathe... Sam." Dr Henderson's words were barely recognisable.

Sam struggled to focus, clamping her eyes shut against the multitude of stimuli and just focussing on Dr Henderson's voice. But even that proved a sensory overload. Her mind's eye projected images of Dr Henderson's face, those beautiful eyes, lips, coming toward her. She could feel the sticky tendrils of desire flowing between them like it was ectoplasm pulling them together simultaneously igniting all her erogenous zones, her mind exploding with arousing images of their hungry mouths, tongues, lips, hands and limbs, touching, caressing, devouring each other.

Sam's body spasmed, arching and flailing like a desperate fish on dry land, in the most violent orgasm possible.

Finally it released her, out of breath, sweating, heavy and spent, back into the chair, exhausted and craving sleep but her body still far too wired to allow it.

---

Victoria watched anxiously, holding her breath, as Sam's body reacted violently, arching repeatedly, causing her to gasp, moan and grit her teeth, obviously fighting for control. After what seemed an eternity, Sam collapsed back in The

Chair, her eyes closed and her breathing measured. Victoria was not sure whether the calm was due to Sam regaining control over her emotions and reactions, or because of sheer exhaustion from what had just happened.

Victoria retreated to the workbench, blind to the vials of the luminous drug and the ongoing distillation process in front of her. She turned around and resolutely braced herself for what she knew she had to do. For extra support she gripped on to the workbench behind her.

She took a deep breath and closed her eyes for a few long seconds.

"You assume too much, Sam. Perhaps I should be clear. I am... not... interested in you. I do... not... want to be near you. I have... no... desire to be kissed, to feel your lips press up against mine." Her tone was measured and chillingly serious.

Victoria knew that under the influence of the drug, if she really felt something for her, hearing this would be an excruciating experience for Sam. Every word would feel like a physical assault igniting the strongest reactions possible in Sam's mind and body.

"I do... not... want our breaths to mingle and our tongues to entwine." Victoria felt self-conscious but continued.

"I do... not... want to feel your breath against my ear, your teeth scraping along my neck. I do... not... want you to undress me, slowly, one button at a time."

Sam strained against her ties, gasping, struggling to control her breathing.

"I do... not... want to feel you take my hard nipple into your mouth, between your teeth, scraping and sucking it. I do... not... want your mouth and tongue trailing slowly down my body, each kiss, each nip pushing me higher... until..."

Sam let out a load moan as her muscles pulled at the restraints.

"Feel it!" Victoria commanded.

Sam moaned and braced against the brutal onslaught.

Victoria swallowed, trying to focus on what had to be done.

"Now, imagine a cube. See it. Feel it... and project it onto the tank," she said.

For a long few heartbeats, she waited, looking between Sam and the tank.

Nothing happened.

"Just like we've done before. Allow yourself to... feel the smooth, cool surfaces, the hard crisp edges, the sharp corners. Want it!"

Suddenly the tank and the whole of the side of The Cage near the tank erupted in flames. The flames quickly spread until it actively consumed about half the perimeter of The Cage.

Instantly Victoria panicked and her first thought was to get Sam and herself out of the burning lab as soon as possible. The flames were quite close to her now.

For some reason she stretched out her hand and felt the flames. They were cool, not hot, and there seemed to be no obvious reason for a fire, no plausible source. She realised that whatever she was seeing had to be a projection, more than likely created by Sam's unconscious, rather than a real fire. A response to the psychological pressure she was experiencing, on account of Victoria's description, must have triggered an abnormal reaction. This caused a thought or emotionally charged memory, possibly one formed under extreme stress, to be revivified and to be manifested. Victoria did not know much about Sam's background, which was a huge drawback for these trials. Unless the Subjects were very young and undamaged or, at the very least, their backgrounds and potential triggers known, it was impossible to even remotely postulate a response to certain stimuli.

Once she had calmed herself down she managed to have a good look around at the flames. Not in her wildest dreams had she believed such a detailed, authentic manifestation possible. She realised that for Sam this situation must be hugely disturbing.

"Stay calm... And breathe," she said in a steady even tone. "Remember whatever is happening is not real. It's just in your mind. It is all an illusion. You are safe. You are in control."

Victoria took a deep breath. She knew she needed to push on and take Sam even further. She licked her dry lips, swallowed and gripped the workbench behind her even harder.

"I do... not... want you..." she said more softly than before. She closed her eyes and sucked in an unsteady breath, holding it for a moment. "... to... take me." Her words were barely audible and dripping with her own desire as they reached Sam's ears.

Sam's body thrust up into the air, letting out a soundless scream as another orgasm raked her body repeatedly before she finally, mercifully collapsed back into The Chair, completely spent.

Behind the one-way mirrored wall, in the Observation room, Jesse paced the floor in the confined space. After just seeing what Sam went through when Dr Henderson injected her with the drug, he really regretted his harsh decision. How could he have agreed to make her believe he deserted her? Yes, he was angry with her that day for putting them all in danger. Yes, he was ready to resign as her P.C.A. but by the morning he had more or less calmed down and gotten over himself when Dr Henderson stopped him on the way to waking Sam.

She had seen the footage from the previous night in Sam's quarters and wanted to know more what they had been discussing. It was her idea to follow through with the illusion that he had resigned as her P.C.A. She thought it would be a good way to break her defences. It was obvious having Jesse backing her up gave Sam a tremendous amount of security and strength. She convinced Jesse that, if they made her think she did not have that support, they would break through to unleashing her power a lot sooner. Dr Henderson had agreed that he would still be kept on the programme in supra P.C.A. capacity. It would be his job to still look out for her and monitor her but the face to face contact would be handled by a rotation of seemingly anonymous orderlies so that she would not have a chance to form an attachment to any of them.

"Dude, I am a laid back kinda guy but, you are even making me tetchy," Anthony's words brought Jesse out of his reverie.

Jesse came to a standstill next to Anthony and watched the CCTV monitor feed from The Cage.

On the screen he saw Dr Henderson walk over to the bench and talk to Sam. He could see Sam beginning to react to what she was saying. Suddenly, Dr Henderson looked slightly panicked for a few moments before she began to talk to Sam again.

It was highly frustrating. The CCTV feed had no sound. He was desperate to know what was going on. He had to know if Sam was okay.

"Why can't we hear anything? What is she saying?" Jesse asked.

"The Obs room is specially insulated and the microphones in The Cage have not been fitted yet. We were only supposed to move to this new Lab in about six weeks, once they'd finished it," Anthony replied. "Because we do not know how her powers will manifest we had to be extra careful how we perceived the events that take place inside. We had to make sure that we are not affected by her potential powers. The CCTV feed is a time delayed feed and, similarly, the sound feed would need to be filtered to prevent a real time engagement with us here in the Obs room."

Jesse, realising there was nothing more he could do, finally pulled up a chair and sat down next to Anthony to watch the monitor.

---

After a long silent moment Victoria opened her eyes and to her own shock and bewilderment Sam was standing a few feet in front of her. Confused Victoria glanced back at The

Chair wanting to understand how Sam could possibly be free.

However, there on The Chair she saw Sam still tied down securely as before. She was lying very still, either asleep or even unconscious. She refocussed on the apparition in front of her. It must be a projection. Victoria could not actually believe her eyes. This was amazing. Could this actually be real? Or was she hallucinating? Had some of the drug come into contact with her own skin? Could she be experiencing her own drug induced hallucination? Or could Sam actually be capable of projecting such a life-like doppelgänger.

The doppelgänger seemed blind to the flames around them. She had her eyes trained on Victoria and, as if sensing Victoria wanted her to approach, she started walking directly towards her, finally coming to a stop only a few inches in front of her.

Victoria found it hard to breath, let alone move with the doppelgänger so close. She waited, dumbfounded, as the doppelgänger slowly leaned forward and ghosted a kiss, so gently on her lips.

The doppelgänger seemed to take the lack of action as encouragement and moved to deepen the kiss. Finally she pulled away only to let Victoria drink in a few gulps of much needed air.

The doppelgänger moved her attention onto Victoria's neck, kissing, sucking and biting down slightly.

Victoria was unable to do otherwise so she relented and gave in to the onslaught. She had fantasised about the feeling of Sam's lips, her touch, her soft caress, on a few occasions. Never in her wildest dreams did she anticipate this. She was not even sure what this was. She surprised herself when she let out a breathy moan of pleasure.

The doppelgänger slowly and methodically ran her hands up Victoria's arms from her wrists to her shoulders and down over the top of her chest to the top button of her blouse, sending shivers down Victoria's spine.

Their eyes met. Slowly the doppelgänger unbuttoned Victoria's blouse, one button at a time exposing her black bra while keeping unwavering eye contact until she reached up for a lace covered breast, cupping it, caressing it and running a thumb over the pert nipple.

Another involuntary gasp escaped Victoria's lips.

The doppelgänger cupped Victoria's other breast causing her to arch into the exquisite touch. She took the nipple under the fabric between her thumb and forefinger and rolled and squeezed it none too gently.

Victoria moaned trying to push her chest forward to force more contact.

Then the doppelgänger slipped her hand inside the bra and pushed the fabric aside before she bent down and circled Victoria's nipple with her tongue finally taking it into her mouth and sucking and biting again all too softly.

Victoria arched back even more, spreading her arms wider on the workbench, momentarily losing her grip and slipping, knocking into the test tubes and kit on the workbench near her.

The doppelgänger trailed first her hands then her lips down Victoria's body. She knelt down in front of her and looked up into Victoria's eyes, as if asking permission, while she slowly undid her trouser button and zip, pulling it open.

Unable to resist, Victoria threw her head back, shut her

eyes and more than willingly gave in to the exquisite inevitable caress.

The peel of the fire alarm was deafening.

"Attention. Fire. Attention. Fire. Please evacuate," the electronic voice echoed through The Cage.

Dr Henderson was wrenched back to reality.

A split second later the sprinkler system kicked in dousing The Cage, but not having much effect on the now blazing real fire which consumed half the wall of instruments, equipment and cabinets and curtains draped around The Cage.

Victoria was aghast and confused. How could that be? Could this fire be real? It had to be, otherwise the fire alarms would not have been triggered. How did that happen?

Jesse was the first to barge into The Cage. He had only looked away from the monitor for a few brief minutes to grab a cup of water from the water cooler and the next thing he knew the fire alarms were blaring. The moment the alarm sounded he immediately reacted on instinct.

"Fire! Get out! Now—" For a moment the words caught in his throat as he tried to make sense of what he saw. There in the flames, Sam knelt in front of Dr Henderson, who was leaning backward over the workbench, partly undressed. What was she doing? How did she get out of her chair? Only minutes before he had been watching the activity in the Lab in the monitor but Sam was then still strapped into The Chair. He could not quite figure out what Dr Henderson was doing leaning back against the workbench. So how did Sam get out of The Chair that quickly? He glanced at The Chair and saw Sam reclining exactly as she had been on the monitor. Two of them? He saw Sam stir in The Chair. He rushed over to her. She seemed unconscious and in a terrible state. He had to get her out of there.

When he looked back at Dr Henderson she was somehow fully dressed and alone. The double was gone! Had he imagined it? Was he going mad?

At that moment Anthony arrived next to him wrenching him back to the crisis at hand – Fire!

Victoria made a beeline for Sam in the Chair. "Okay, wheel her out. No time to untie," Victoria commanded over the raging noise of the fire.

Victoria helped Jesse flatten The Chair completely, into a reclining position, disengage the brakes, and start to push it toward the door. All three took hold of The Chair and pushed a now groggy, bewildered looking Sam toward the large hall doors.

Suddenly Victoria stopped and turned back to The Cage. Jesse could see the flames starting to lick at the glass tubes on the workbench.

"There's no time! It's going to blow!" Jesse shouted.

"I know, but I have to get—" Victoria replied.

Jesse knew he had to make a choice, save Sam or worry about what Dr Henderson needed.

He knew his job. He redoubled his efforts to push Sam and The Chair out of the hangar as quickly as possible. They had to get beyond the double doors. He could see the fire curtain, that was intended to isolate the hangar from the rest of the institute in case of a fire such as this, was lowering and about a third of the way down already.

Sam must have been awake enough to realise what was going on. When she saw Victoria double back she grew hysterical, pulling and yanking at her restraints, frantic to get loose.

Finally they squeezed under the lowering fire door with just enough room for The Chair to pass, and barged through the double doors into the corridor, but before the doors could swing closed behind them, a large explosion erupted inside the hangar.

Jesse instinctively threw himself over Sam, shielding her with his body as they were propelled farther down the corridor by the blast pushing its way in through the gap still left in the fire curtain.

Once Sam realised what had just happened, she erupted into a blood curdling scream "Victoria! No!"

---

## 14

A General in uniform, accompanied by four soldiers, marched right past Margery and headed into Director Morten's office.

"Wait! Stop!" Margery said jumping up from her seat and rushing after them. "You can't go in there. This is Director Morten's office—"

The General headed to the teak desk where she slowly and methodically removed her gloves and dropped them neatly on the desk. "This is now my office," she replied turning back to face Margery who had finally caught up with them and was also now standing in the middle of Morten's office.

Margery's jaw dropped slightly. The General was Lady Frost!

The thought that Lady Frost could be anything other than an influential, probably wealthy Cougar who liked to play sugar mummy to Director Morten would never have occurred to Margery.

Lady Frost walked right up to Margery, invading her personal space.

Margery could not help feeling like a deer between headlights.

"Margery, is it?" Lady Frost purred.

Margery suddenly found her mouth very dry. She nodded.

Lady Frost smiled a warm, calming smile.

Margery surmised that that was one of Lady Frost's arsenal of devices which she used to expertly manipulate and influence people. Although she was adamant not to be manipulated, she did feel a sense of ease descend over her.

"Margery, please can you hold all my calls and get Mr Morten for me."

Lady Frost's words were so gentle and earnest, that before she knew it, Margery nodded and scuttled away to do as she had been asked.

Lady Frost turned to the soldiers. "I want the Subject secured, the new lab cleared and a full update on the takeover status."

"Yes, sir," one of the soldiers replied.

"Good. Dismissed." Lady Frost turned and headed to the desk.

The soldiers saluted and left.

---

Morten entered his office, holding a freshly made mug of coffee, unaware of the new situation. When he saw Lady Frost sitting behind his desk reading through some reports he was bewildered and delighted.

"I didn't know you were stopping by," he said reaching to close the door.

"No, leave that open," she said, getting up to help herself to water from the decanter on the drinks cabinet.

Morten left the door. Only then, while Lady Frost was standing at the cabinet pouring herself a drink, did he notice her new attire.

"Oh, I like the outfit." He feasted his eyes on her lean, shapely body accentuated by the masculine cut of the uniform. "I've always had a thing for women in uniform." The fact that it was a General's uniform had completely escaped him.

"Hugo, the board is not pleased," Lady Frost continued in a business-like manner. "They want a full audit… and The ADV Programme back up and running… yesterday."

"I said we'd need a week to recruit a new head of research," Morten explained, about to take a sip of his coffee but deciding it was too hot.

"Report!" Lady Frost commanded, startling Morten. He looked round to find two soldiers entering the office behind him. Morten was about to object when one stepped forward, ignoring Morten completely and addressing Lady Frost. "Lab and Subject secured, General."

The implication of the last word slowly filtered into Morten's consciousness.

"General?" He was not sure he had heard that right. "Since when?"

Lady Frost briefly turned her attention back to him. "A new head of research will not be necessary."

She continued to address the soldiers. "Please fetch Sergeant Elms for me."

The soldiers saluted and left.

"Sergeant... Elms?" Morten was beginning to question whether he was in some kind of surreal dream state or alternative reality.

"Yes, he has assured me he's fully briefed in all areas of The ADV Programme and able to recommence the programme right away."

"Yes, but he's—"

"Effective immediately," Lady Frost announced.

The first thing that struck Jesse, on his first day back on the job, was that the facility was overrun with soldiers swarming all over the place.

After the previous fiasco in The Cage, wherein he, Sam and Anthony had barely come out alive, they were all rushed to the infirmary and after about six hours of tests and observation he was sent home to recover on compulsory leave. That was ten days ago.

Jesse was not happy about having to leave Sam. He was very worried about her. After everything she had been through he wanted to be there for her. He could only imagine what she must be going through.

He had so many questions but none he could officially get any answers to. He had been told that his charge had been 'decommissioned' and as a result he did not have the clearance for anything on the ADV Programme any longer.

He absolutely did need to know if Sam was safe so, despite his lack of clearance, he managed to blag his way into the ADV area saying that if he was no longer needed as a

P.C.A. for the Subject, he needed to fetch some highly classified reports from the Lab and make sure they got handed over to his colleagues.

In the meantime, the whole facility was buzzing with rumour and speculation about why the military had moved in, what had happened during the incident that day and whether anyone had been seriously hurt. He understood why the powers that be would prefer to keep the whole thing under wraps, officially holding the line that it was merely an unscheduled fire drill. If the truth about an incident of that magnitude and what had really happened got out, it would certainly cause a huge corporate and public outcry, especially once it became known that their star researcher and co-founder Dr Henderson had died in the blast. So far, he had no idea what had really happened, or whether there was any chance Dr Henderson could have survived. He was hoping Anthony would tell him more.

Jesse entered what was left of the hangar where The Cage had been constructed, to find, to his great surprise, that it had been cleaned up and seemed to be back in operation, with no sign of the fire and explosion.

If anything he was expecting to see Sam in position in The Chair. He had already resolved that if they had started on her trials again he would approach Director Morten and insist that she needed more rest and recovery time.

Hence, he was even more surprised to see no sign of Sam, but instead a dozen gurneys occupied by twelve men in uniform. They were positioned four in a row, in three lines, in the middle of The Cage. Each soldier had fitted what looked like an upgraded version of the headset and goggles like the one Dr Elms had used on Sam before Dr Henderson intervened. In the middle of them Jesse saw Dr Elms, now also in military uniform. He was observing the soldiers, taking notes and barking orders at Anthony who was trying to man the large new instrument panel – an upgrade from the small controls that were on the portable bust stand of the goggles previously used on Sam.

"Fast forward S-zero-four to the Phobia set," Dr Elms said.

Anthony inserted a disk into a slot in the control panel and adjusted a dial.

Jesse headed over to stand near Anthony so that he could talk to him without Dr Elms hearing.

"Wow! And this?" he whispered to Anthony slightly nodding his head in the direction of Dr Elms and the soldiers.

"Who knew," Anthony replied under his breath.

"S-zero-five to Elemental set," came Dr Elms' next command. Anthony adjusted the dial.

Jesse focussed on the real reason he had come to see Anthony. "Where is Sam?" he asked in another whisper.

"Sedated." Anthony guessed Jesse's next question. "In the Lab."

"Why?" This did not make sense to Jesse. Why, after all that, would they now sedate her? He understood they would probably need to reassess the data and figure out what caused the incident before they progressed with her trials, but sedating her, that was a surprise.

"S-zero-six to Irrationals set zero two." Dr Elms barked out.

He then suddenly became aware of Jesse's presence.

"Orderly Wyatte, your services will not be required here today."

"Yes, Dr Elms," Jesse replied. "I'll go make myself useful elsewhere."

Anthony jabbed Jesse with his elbow. At first Jesse did not know what he meant. Then he realised. "Useful elsewhere, sir," he corrected himself.

"I'll explain in a minute," Anthony quickly whispered, nodding to the door to indicate Jesse should leave and wait outside.

Jesse headed to the door.

Dr Elms seemed satisfied that Jesse was leaving and turned his attention back to the next soldier.

"S-zero-seven through to S-twelve control sets."

"Yes, sir." Anthony said. "Done, sir."

"Good. Now get me the files from the Lab."

Dr Elms had certainly found his stride with giving orders, Jesse thought.

"Yes, sir," Anthony replied.

What was with the sir thing? Jesse thought.

"And don't forget the recordings," Dr Elms said.

"I won't, Dr Elms," Anthony replied.

"Sergeant... Elms," Dr Elms corrected.

"Sorry. Sergeant Elms, sir," Anthony replied before he headed out of The Cage.

---

Jesse waited for Anthony just outside the swinging doors to the corridor. He had so many questions and not very much time.

Finally Anthony pushed through the double doors.

Jesse fell in step next to him as they headed to the Lab.

"They don't want her starting up another fire," Anthony explained pre-empting Jesse's question.

"They think she really did that?" Jesse was stunned. "Rather than it being an accident?"

Anthony nodded.

"And what happened to Dr Henderson?" Jesse asked. "Is the rumour true? Or did she survive?"

Anthony dropped his head, suddenly finding it easier to look at his feet as they walked along.

"Yes," he said. "They intend to make a public announcement in the next few weeks. They want the military to settle in place first, with their take over, before they go public so that they can say that the military have everything under control now."

Jesse's heart sank. Oh my. "Does Sam know?"

Anthony shrugged his shoulders. "I have not seen very much of her since the medical. I was sent home on 24 hour recovery which was then cut short 18 hours later so I could take up position under Elms as he took over the Programme. And I have not really had time to breathe since, never mind ask questions."

As they approached the Lab, Jesse saw that there were two soldiers standing guard outside the door. He should have expected that.

"This is Orderly Jesse Wyatte," Anthony informed the guards. "He's the Subject's P.C.A., we are here to monitor her progress."

One of the guards checked their name badges and finally stepped aside to let them pass.

Once inside the Lab, Jesse had to resist the incredibly overpowering impulse to rush up to Sam's side where she lay on a gurney, motionless, clearly heavily sedated. She looked so thin and pale and Jesse's heart went out to her. It was clear they had probably kept her constantly sedated since the incident in The Cage.

Instead, Jesse followed Anthony into the Observation Room. He had to get as much information as possible about what was happening from Anthony.

Once inside the Observation room Jesse pulled out his Psych Eval folder, as much as a result of habit as a way to divert his attention from Anthony who he feared might otherwise get spooked and realise that he probably should not divulge so much to Jesse.

Despite Anthony being focussed on rounding up the files and disks he needed for Dr Elms, he noticed what Jesse was doing. "Bet you're glad you won't have to do that for a while," Anthony said raising his eyebrows at the file in Jesse's hand.

Jesse nodded. "How long do they plan on keeping her sedated?"

Anthony's pager beeped.

He read the message.

"SERGEANT Elms is going to make my blood boil, soon," he said, replacing his pager in his pocket.

"Until she is no longer a threat at least. The drug has an eight week half-life and we don't know exactly at what point it'll no longer pose a problem."

"What? So you're going to keep her sedated for eight weeks?" Jesse said, trying not to sound too alarmed.

"Not me, mate." Anthony lifted his hands in surrender. "But yes. They probably will, just to be sure we don't have any more incidents."

"Was anything recovered from the cameras that could explain how the fire started?" Jesse asked.

Anthony finally seemed to have gathered everything he needed.

"All the disks fried in the fire." Anthony shook his head. "They had to rebuild the whole of The Cage and the Observation Ro—"

Anthony's pager beeped again causing him to grumble. He read it and went to retrieve another file from his desk drawer.

"So now what happens to Sam once the drug is no longer a problem?" Jesse felt pressurised. He needed more time with Anthony. "Reset her and let her loose in the world to fend for herself like some discarded trash?"

"If only," Anthony remarked. "I'm afraid your charge is now a highly sought after military asset. They'll find a use for her skills, whether she likes it or not." There was a long silence and finally Anthony looked up and read his thoughts. It must come as a great shock to find out one's charge, someone you have been sworn to protect and look out for, is as good as dead or, if not, destined to a life in torturous slavery.

"Really sorry, mate."

Anthony's pager beeped again.

"Look, I really have to go. I suspect you probably want to

check in on her but I need to get these back to Elms before I end up one of his lab rats myself."

Jesse felt very grateful. He realised that, under the circumstances, it was an immense gesture of trust for Anthony to suggest he could check up on Sam, unsupervised.

Anthony grabbed the enormous pile of folders and disks, and headed for the door. On his way Anthony dropped one of the disks.

"Ant, you dropped..." he said as he reached over and picked it up but Anthony had already disappeared out the door.

Jesse studied the disk in his hand. It was labelled "Erotic Set 01". He resolved to give it to Anthony later and popped it into his pocket.

He decided he would update the Psych Eval report before he went in to see Sam, regardless, even if that meant just adding in the dates since the incident and recording that she has been sedated. He sat down at the table in front of the glass.

As he opened the folder an A4 sized photograph stared back at him. At first he could not figure it out. Then he realised that it was a photograph of The Cage from the aerial perspective of a CCTV camera on the day of the incident. He picked it up to find two more nearly identical photographs underneath. He could see Dr Henderson standing at the workbench and Sam reclining in The Chair on the other side of The Cage.

What would these be doing in his Psych Eval file? He remembered Anthony said there was no footage of the incident. So where did these come from? Was someone trying to tell him something? Why would they tell him? The gnawing sensation in his gut turned into an ache in his chest. Someone … who knew he would look out for Sam. He did not fully understand why, but he suddenly knew Sam was in danger and it was up to him to help her. He could not let her be taken prisoner, or treated like a lab rat, again, by the Military.

He had to get her out of there.

With that, Jesse was galvanised into action. Now was probably going to be his only chance to get near Sam; so, he had to move fast, and move now!

He grabbed the folder and headed into the Lab.

## 15

Inside the lab Jesse briefly checked Sam's vitals. He was right. She had been heavily sedated and she looked even worse on closer examination but he could not let that affect him right now. He had very little time before the guards would become suspicious.

He headed to the wall of cabinets and began to search through them. Each Lab in the facility had its own store of emergency drugs, which was quite extensive, so he knew they would have what he needed, he just had to find it. Finally he recognised the small 5ml glass bottle containing the clear liquid. He read the label: flumazenil.

He rummaged in a draw and found a sterilised dispenser. He ripped it out of its packaging. As he loaded the dispenser he noticed his hands were trembling. He had no time to be nervous now. Sam depended on him.

Once back at Sam's side he took hold of her arm and, without even sterilising the skin, punched the dispenser onto the crook of her elbow. His attention was drawn once more to how small and frail her arms had become due to lack of food and muscular atrophy.

He checked his watch. He was not sure how he was going to pull this off but he had to try.

To the side of the room, near Sam's feet, stood a large, 3 panel, concertina modesty screen, which, although it seemed standard in all the Labs, had so far been of very little use during Sam's trials.

Jesse grabbed the modesty screen and wheeled it into place so that it shielded Sam, as best as possible, from the view of the guards through the vision-panel, the Observation room and the CCTV cameras situated in the corner of the Lab. If anyone ever looked back at the CCTV footage it would no doubt be easy to see what he was doing but that did not concern him now. He just needed to buy himself enough time, without rousing suspicion, to get Sam out of there.

He checked his watch again and impatiently rubbed Sam's hand, willing her to regain consciousness quicker.

"Come on! Sam, can you hear me?" he whispered.

He nervously glanced at the Observation window and the Lab door.

Through the vision-panel in the door he could see one of the guards. Luckily they had their head turned away and seemed to be engaged in conversation with his mate.

For his plan to work Jesse needed a vehicle, ideally something wherein Sam could hide.

He searched the room for inspiration. Then he spotted the cupboard trolley he had used so many times before to transport equipment and supplies to and from the Lab. He pulled it up close to the gurney, making sure it was hidden from view, behind the screen, and engaged the brakes.

"Sam!" he whispered more urgently this time. "Sam, if you can hear me, you've got to listen to me. We have to get you out of here."

To his relief, Sam moaned softly.

"Sam? Thank God! You've got to wake up. We have to get you out of here. This is our only chance."

Sam stirred. "Jess..."

"Come on. We don't have much time."

"No." Her voice was soft and groggy from not using it for such a long time. "I killed her. They are right…"

Jesse did not understand what she was saying, but right now was not the time to engage in conversation.

"I'm dangerous," she finally said.

"Sam, just listen to me." Jesse needed to get his message across as quickly and clearly as possible. He really could have done without her stubbornness at this point. He realised she felt responsible for what happened to Dr Henderson. Somehow she must have found out that Dr Henderson had died in the incident.

"The Military have taken over. They will turn you into a weapon, if they even let you live. Dr H would not have wanted that! Now come on!"

Sam trusted Jesse with her life. She tried to move. Her body felt like lead. Her head pulsed like it was about to explode and her mouth was parched with cracked lips. The effects of the drug Dr Henderson had given her were far from worn off – all her senses were still acutely sensitised. Even the slightest stimulus, like where Jesse gently held her shoulder to encourage her to sit up was excruciating. She was not sure she was actually capable of going anywhere.

"I can't," she finally confessed.

"Yes, you can. I saw that thing you did—your, your double. Do you think you can do it again?" He opened the doors to the trolley. "We need to get you in here—"

There was a rap on the vision-panel of the Lab door. One of the guards, the larger of the two, who checked their identity earlier, pushed through the door. "What's taking so long?"

Jesse swiftly jumped out from behind the screen, pulling a face.

He reached over and grabbed a huge wad of paper towelling and a bedpan from the cabinet making a big display of his disgust.

"Ugh, jeez man! It's so unpleasant when a catheter bag rips. I won't be long. Just got to clean her up again otherwise she'll stink us all out."

The soldier swallowed, clearly repulsed by the idea and certainly not wanting to get involved. "Okay, but make it quick."

Jesse ducked back behind the screen to find Sam lying very still once again. He feared that she had slipped back into unconsciousness.

"Sam! Come on! We've got to move." He shook her gently.

"Down here." Sam's pained voice drifted up from inside the trolley cupboard.

Jesse realised that it was her doppelgänger on the gurney and he recoiled like he had just touched a dead person. He struggled to believe his eyes and took another good look at the doppelgänger, poking it briefly. A noise at the door however re-focussed him. He put the bedpan on the trolley and stuffed the paper towel into it.

"Okay, don't look now," he whispered.

Jesse unzipped his trousers and peed on the paper towel. He zipped up.

He bent down and peered into the trolley to find Sam lying scrunched up in the confined space, clearly in great agony and trying to control her breathing. He grabbed the Psych Eval file from where he had dropped it on the side of the gurney and stuffed it into the bottom of the trolley under her bent knees.

"Okay you ready? Think you can maintain Sammy junior here for long enough till we're past the guards?"

Sam did not respond. He hoped that she heard and understood the plan. He closed the trolley door leaving only a small gap to allow in enough air for Sam to breathe.

Here goes nothing, he thought as he pushed the trolley toward the door, glancing back one last time to make sure Sam's double was still in place.

---

At the door the shorter, tubbier of the two soldiers who to this point had still not said a word, stepped in front of the trolley.

"Jeez, man! You can be glad you don't have my job, I can assure you!" Jesse said.

"Open," the other soldier said, reaching down to grab the trolley doors.

"I would really not do that if I were you," Jesse said swiftly halting the soldier mid move.

"What's in it?" he asked.

"A lot more of this," Jesse said indicating the bedpan and its contents. Had to give her a change of clothes. Again Jesse made sure to drive the displeasure home by showing the disgust on his face and turning away bracing himself from the potential stench that would follow if the guard continued to open the doors.

"Besides, what am I going to smuggle out of there? Certainly not The Flame-thrower herself. I might have a shit job but I'm not suicidal," Jesse said.

The soldier hesitated, looking at his mate for support.

"Have a look in the Lab if you don't believe me. Can we just hurry? Because I'm covered in pee and need to get this over with as soon as possible."

The taller soldier went to the vision-panel and peeped inside, confirming that Sam was still lying on the bed, partly obscured by the modesty screen. He nodded at his mate. "She's in there alright. You can let him through."

"Thanks," Jesse said and began to push onward down the corridor. "Oh, and I'd stay well clear, if I were you. Obviously I could not fully bathe her," Jesse threw back over his shoulder as continued to put as much distance between them, as fast as possible.

---

They needed to go somewhere private, somewhere where he could stop and think through how to get Sam out of the facility undetected.

It was one thing getting her past the guards out of the Lab. It would be quite another trying to get her out of the facility. There was no knowing what the consequences of getting caught would be, however he was pretty sure it did not bear thinking about.

Up ahead, on the corridor to the right, he saw the door to a storeroom that he was pretty sure would not get much traffic. He headed straight for it.

Luckily it was for general supplies and his access card still worked.

Once inside he closed the door securely behind them. He also pulled up a cleaning trolley and jammed it in front of the door to barricade it in case someone did decide to come knocking.

Then he wheeled the trolley farther into what was, now, not much more than a large supply cupboard. It must have been a Lab or Subject room at some stage because it still had a small hand basin, a mirror on the wall and a hospital bed in one corner. The rest of the space was mostly used as a storage area for extra cleaning equipment and to house old filling cabinets.

Jesse parked the trolley and engaged the brakes. He opened the doors.

Sam was still curled inside the trolley in obvious agony. He did not know whether it was better to leave her or help her out. In the end he decided she would be better off in one of the wheelchairs that were also stored in the storeroom.

Once he had secured the wheelchair and lifted her out of the cupboard, he realised that by the time they headed out of there everyone would be out looking for her.

"We've got to disguise you somehow," he said, thinking

fast as he scanned the storeroom. On the shelf he spotted an electric razor. He grabbed it and manoeuvred the wheelchair so that Sam could face the small mirror on the wall.

"It grows back," he said, in case she harboured any objection. "Believe me, everyone here knows about the blond Flame-thrower and if they see me with you, we are toast."

"Jess, you should take me back." Her voice was very weak and strained with pain. "I'm dangerous. This power is dangerous. I killed her."

Jesse noticed the tears running down Sam's cheeks.

"That is exactly why we have to get you out of here! The Military will use you to do far worse, believe me." He suddenly remembered the photographs. "Besides," he grabbed the file from the trolley cupboard and placed it on Sam's lap, "I found these in my Psych Eval folder."

With shaking hands and determined effort Sam opened the file. She instantly recognised the photographs. "What are these? Are you trying to punish me?" she asked weakly, not able to understand why Jesse would present her with harrowing reminders of that day.

"No, no! According to Anthony there was never any footage recovered from the camera's in The Cage."

"So?"

"So... How could these exist?" Jesse asked. "And why are they in my Psych Eval file?"

Sam studied the photographs for a long moment while Jesse proceeded to shave her head. "That's odd," she finally said.

"What?" Jesse remained focussed on the task at hand not wanting to accidentally cause her any more pain.

"The vial, it has moved," Sam explained.

The top photograph depicted an aerial shot of The Cage, showing Sam strapped in the chair and Dr Henderson next to the workbench facing Sam. A small vial, which Sam recognised as the same drug Dr Henderson had injected into her, stood on the workbench next to Dr Henderson's right hand a little way off from the other glass tubes and chemistry paraphernalia.

The middle photograph was almost identical to the first in all respects except Dr Henderson was now leaning backward over the workbench, her arms bracing herself farther apart with her head thrown back and her lips parted. Vivid memories of the incident hit Sam like a torrent of physical blows simultaneously excruciatingly painful and immensely arousing. She shook her head in an attempt to refocus.

Flipping back to the first photograph she said, "Here it is next to the Doc."

Then she tapped the second photograph in the spot where the vial was lying in the middle of the workbench. "But here is it lying in the middle of the table."

She flipped to the third, almost identical, photograph wherein the vial was now gone completely from the table and a fire was visible on the floor on the opposite side of the workbench. "And there it's gone."

She tried to brace herself against the racking effects as more vivid, involuntary memory flashes flooded her senses — Dr Henderson's partly naked torso, Sam's outstretched hand caressing her soft breast, Dr Henderson looking down at her, gasping, and arching, pressing into her hand, needing more.

Just then Sam remembered Dr Henderson's hold slipping

on the edge of the table knocking something over next
to her.

"She must have knocked the vial over and when it rolled
off the workbench it ignited the fire," Sam said weakly.

Jesse peered over her shoulder to take a better look.

"She said it was highly volatile. That's why she had to
strap me in," Sam said.

"Enough to cause a fire like that?"

"I think so, possibly."

"That's great! So you're not dangerous." Jesse said with
some initial relief. "At least not in the way we thought you
were. Now we just need to get you out of here without
moving you, so you don't self-combust. This just keeps
getting better."

Sam shook her head. "It might not have been my power
that started the fire but it was still my actions that caused it."

"What are you talking about?"

"I distracted her." Tears ran down Sam's cheeks once
more. "You were right I pushed, too far, and only ever
thought about what I wanted."

Vivid, excruciating memories of her ripping open Dr
Henderson's trousers and Dr Henderson arching into the
caress flashed through her mind. Feelings of arousal mixed
with devastation, anguish, grief and shame, tore through her
body, amplified a hundred fold.

"I have to go back," she said with steely resolve.

"What?" For a moment Jesse thought he had not heard
correctly. "No way! I've just risked my hide to get you out of
there. There is no way I'm going to help you back in!" He
could see the determination in her eyes and marvelled at
how, even in her weakened state, she could be so stubborn.

"Why?" he asked finally, hoping that reason would help convince her otherwise.

"I have to make it right. I have to destroy the drug," she said simply. "Dr H would not have wanted the Military to have the drug."

"You can hardly walk—"

"If you won't help me I'll do it on my own."

Jesse held Sam's unwavering gaze. Finally he shook his head. "You do push," he concluded with a shake of the head.

Jesse swiftly rifled through the filing cabinets in the storeroom and grabbed the first Subject file he could find. He popped it on Sam's lap. Then he pushed the cleaning trolley aside, wheeled her out into the corridor where they headed back into the lion's den.

## 16

Jesse pushed Sam back toward the ADV Programme security checkpoint through which he had managed to smuggle her out, less than an hour ago, in the belly of the trolley.

"They're certainly giving you the run around today, mate," Corporal Rheems said taking the file from Jesse's outstretched hand and scanning it quickly.

"You have no idea." Jesse answered hoping his nerves would not let him down. "This is my new one."

"Yeah, I believe the last one got a bit too hot to handle," Corporal Rheems said with a chuckle.

Something caught his attention in the file. Jesse mentally kicked himself. He should have checked the details of the Subject file before they left the storeroom to make sure it fitted Sam's description.

"Paul Sebothelo?" Corporal read the name of the new Subject, then looked at Jesse, confused, "of African descent?"

Oh shit! Jesse thought as he and the Corporal stared down at a sleeping Sam who was far more likely from a

Scandinavian bloodline with her blond hair and moderately fair skin.

"Who knew?" Jesse said and shrugged his shoulders and looked Corporal Rheems straight in the eye. There was a long pause. Jesse could see Corporal Rheems capitulate. Then, to his relief, Rheems shrugged his shoulders. "When you have worked here a while, just when you think you have seen it all, then a new one comes along." He handed Jesse back his file. "Good luck with this one," he said as he waved them through.

Jesse and Sam headed along the corridors trying to avoid anyone who would be able to recognise either of them. Luckily, her time at PhyCorp had been limited to Lab work and only a handful of Orderlies and Technician had worked with her. Similarly, he had been so busy looking after her that he had had very little time to fraternise with any staff beyond Dr Henderson's core team. It also helped that since the Military had taken over, the PhyCorp staff had been reduced by half, however, now there were soldiers on almost every corridor so they could not let their guard down.

"I don't remember seeing it in the Lab," Jesse said, referring to the drug, "only in the Cage that day."

"I'm pretty certain the drug would be under lock and key. She knew its power and Dr Henderson would have made a point to keep it somewhere safe," Sam said, "Probably somewhere no one else would have easy access to it. Not even Elms or Morten." Sam thought about it for a moment. "Can you get me to her office?"

Jesse looked incredulous. "What?"

"I remember there were a couple of filing cabinets in the corner," Sam said.

Jesse could not believe what she was proposing. "Dr Henderson's office is most likely the best guarded area of the entire institute, other than the Lab you were kept in."

"You got me out of there didn't you?" Sam said.

To Jesse's surprise the corridors leading up to the Administration Wing were quite deserted with only one or two soldiers patrolling. It was fairly easy to make up a reason when they were heading in that direction, which did not involve actually saying they were going to the Administration Wing.

Then, they were about to turn the final corner when they heard voices coming from up ahead.

Jesse stopped pushing the wheelchair, sidestepping it to peer around the corner.

A final security check point had been set up just outside the main gate to the Administration Wing, complete with two uncannily similar looking soldiers. The voices belonged to Dr Elms and one of the soldiers who was letting him through at that moment.

"Shit!" Jesse said. Just their luck that Elms had beaten them to it. What now? Turn back? Sam would not want to turn back.

Suddenly he become aware of voices coming up from behind them too.

"I have an idea." Sam said. "Just go through the gate."

"What?"

"Trust me. Just keep going. Push me to the security gate and follow my lead!"

"But Sam—"

"Just do it. We don't have time," she urged.

Jesse grabbed hold of the chair, took a deep breath hoping Sam knew what she was doing.

---

The two soldiers observed them suspiciously when they approached the gate.

"Evening." Jesse tried to keep his tone light. "I—"

"Nobody is allowed through here." The one soldier stepped forward.

Jesse noticed both their name badges said "Timm."

"I know, ah—"

Just then Jesse saw a silhouette appear in the corridor behind the soldiers on the other side of the gate, more or less in line with Dr Henderson's open office door. His heart sank. That is all they need. To have Dr Elms discover them. He would most certainly recognise him and Sam. He felt himself inwardly cringe and brace against the events to follow.

"Come on! Hurry up!" Dr Elms barked. "I don't have all day."

Jesse froze, not understanding what was going on. Then he felt Sam nudge the chair as if to make it go. He followed her lead and pushed on answering swiftly, "Yes, sir."

The two soldiers both seemed as startled by Dr Elms' appearance but reacted promptly and hurried to open the gate to let Jesse and Sam through.

"Sorry, Sergeant. We didn't realise they were—" the one Timm started to say.

"And do not let anyone else through!" Dr Elms barked once more. "Not without my say so!"

At that point Jesse could have sworn he saw Dr Elms flicker slightly like some ghostly apparition. He glanced round at the soldiers to see if they had noticed. They both glanced at each other. He was pretty sure they noticed it too.

"Got that?" Dr Elms said.

"Yes, sir. Understood, sir." The soldiers turned back taking up their posts.

Jesse guessed that soldiers must sometimes be expected to turn a blind eye, to a number of things, in the line of duty. In a place like this that was probably not an unusual occurrence.

Jesse pushed Sam swiftly toward Dr Henderson's office.

---

As Jesse and Sam approached the open door to Dr Henderson's office they could hear metal scraping and hollow banging coming from inside. Once they got close enough to look around the corner they saw Dr Elms inside intently focussed on trying to jemmy open the locked set of filing cabinets with a crow bar.

Jesse very quietly parked Sam's wheelchair just inside the office, out of sight of the Timms. He put his finger up to his lips to show Sam to be as quiet as possible. He was hoping Dr Elms was too focussed on the cabinets to notice them behind him, not too much of a stretch considering he obviously had not noticed the commotion in the hall outside a few minutes ago.

Jesse pushed past the wheelchair quietly and sneaked up behind Dr Elms. In one swift punch he jabbed Dr Elms in the neck with the tranquilliser ring, which was still on his finger from when Dr Elms had originally given it to him to use on Sam.

It took a split second before Dr Elms collapsed backward without a sound in slow motion, unconscious, into Jesse's outstretched arms.

With a hand under each armpit Jesse dragged him over to Dr Henderson's chair and propped him up behind the desk.

"I bet that was satisfying," Sam whispered, smiling slightly.

"Yes, been wanting to give him a bit of his own medicine for a while," Jesse whispered back.

Jesse made swift work of placing the ring on Dr Elms' finger and repositioning his pose to make it look like he'd injected himself and collapsed forward onto the desk.

"Will he be okay?" Sam asked.

"He'll be out cold for a couple of hours, then he'll wake up with the mother of all hangovers and be unable to remember a thing about the past six months."

Jesse went to close the office door quietly behind Sam.

"Okay. So you reckon Dr H might have kept the drug here in her office? Any idea where to start looking?" he asked.

"I'm pretty sure they'll be here somewhere," Sam said scanning the room. "Elms seemed pretty convinced that something was hidden here."

Jesse headed over to the open cabinets and began to flit through the documents. "These are just old stocktaking and payroll records."

Finally he pulled out a personnel file. "Here I am." He studied it briefly before he placed it on the edge of the desk.

Jesse glanced at the bookshelf. He noticed the time on the wall clock read 12:34. "We'd better hurry. They might not have noticed you missing yet but my absence will start sounding alarm bells soon."

"I just need a little more time," Sam said also trying to survey the bookshelf from her seat in the wheelchair. She felt frustrated by her lack of strength. It was very hard to participate effectively in a world from the perspective of most people's navels.

"Okay, well, if it gets to it I might have to nip back while you stay here." Jesse was very reluctant to leave Sam but realised that if he was missed then all sorts of alarm bells would sound and he did not want to risk them checking the Lab and discovering Sam missing on his account. "At least Timm and Timm are not likely to come and bother you any time soon."

"Will you be okay? I'll come to get you as soon as I can." Sam nodded.

As he was about to disappear out the door she caught his wrist. "Thank you... for everything," she said looking him straight in the eye. She did not want to think what would have been her fate had Jesse walked out on her those weeks ago. She was very lucky to have such a friend.

Jesse nodded and slipped out closing the door behind him. Sam could hear the voices come from the corridor as Jesse conversed with Timm and Timm.

Jesse approached the gate where Timm and Timm were standing guard. Without having to ask them Timm swiftly opened the gate to let him out.

"He's a bit touchy today," Jesse said. "I wouldn't disturb him if I were you!"

———

Sam braced herself and with all her might pushed against the armrests of the wheelchair to raise herself. It felt like she was a baby learning to stand for the first time. The pain resulting from the over sensitivity to any stimulation, caused by the drugs in her system, was one thing. That she could somehow deal with. The problem was the complete lack of strength. After much effort she pushed herself up out of the wheelchair and made her way, on very wobbly legs, toward the bookshelf. She was too weak and had to support herself and rest frequently on the furniture and against the wall along the way.

Finally, by clinging onto the bookshelf, she traversed along it studying the various book titles as she went. She noticed the same small crew lantern she remembered from that evening when she came to see Dr Henderson. Suddenly she felt overwhelmed by remorse. Jesse was right, she did push. She wanted Victoria so badly she was blind to the consequences and how much danger that put Victoria in. If she really cared about Victoria she should never have volunteered for this programme in the first place. She should have left her well alone. She did not deserve this. Even if it did not end in tragedy, as it had, Victoria never deserved her with all her baggage and troubles. She could never have offered anything.

But, sadly, she had to face the fact that she could not go back and fix the past right now. In the same way she could not go back and rescue her Unit after the event, as much as she had wished she could do many things very differently. The past is the past.

The only thing left for her now was to fix the present. That she could still do.

She gritted her teeth. Come on Victoria. What do you care about? Where would you keep your most precious secrets? She thought.

She glanced around the room and her eye landed on the picture of Florence Nightingale on the wall.

There were no other pictures or images of family or friends anywhere to be seen, yet she had a picture of Nightingale on the wall. Sam hobbled over to it.

She inspected it, running her fingers along the wooden frame. When she found nothing she carefully lifted it away from the wall and peeped behind it.

"Ah. There you are," She said quietly to herself, a small smile curling her lips.

There, tucked away, hidden behind Florence Nightingale's austere facade lay a hidden treasure, a small, metal safe.

Sam gripped the frame of the picture and lifted it off its hook in the wall.

The safe was a simple keyed lock box, set into the wall, about 50cm by 50cm in size.

Sam fingered the keyhole as she considered the room once more.

"Now where would you hide it?" she said. "Somewhere easy to get to... but where you'd be pretty sure no one would look."

Her eyes fell on Dr Henderson's desk. Too obvious, she thought. Besides, judging by their half open and tousled appearance it looked like Dr Elms had already thoroughly combed through each drawer.

Her gaze roamed across the contents of the bookshelf landing, finally, on the little silver lantern once more.

Could that be the Lady's lamp?

She made her way over to it.

She picked it up and examined it from all angles.

The little door had a metal plaque on it with the inscription:

"I am a man of action." — Florence Nightingale (1820 – 1910)

Sam glanced back at the Florence Nightingale picture.

"Could that be it?" Sam said as a small smile formed on her lips.

It made sense that Florence Nightingale was a prominent influence on Dr Henderson. The key had to be here somewhere.

Sam inspected the lantern thoroughly. She opened the little door and took out the large metal tea light inside it. As she lowered it, she noticed that the tea light's opaque white candle had two wicks, one black from being burnt and the other still white.

Near her, on the shelf, she noticed a small wax cloth and on it a lighter. Sam reached for it and flicked the lighter. It worked.

She brought the small lighter flame over to the lantern and lit the blackened wick before she replaced it in the lantern. "Here goes nothing," she said quietly.

She was not sure what would happen. She had somehow expected something theatrical, like the flame of the lantern to cast a secret shadow or illuminate some hidden message, to reveal the location of the key. She was beginning to think it was a stupid idea.

She wait a little longer, studying the rest of the bookshelf.

Had she missed something else?

Most of the books in the bookshelves were old medical journals but nothing that leapt out at her.

Finally she returned to the lantern, conceding that she had it all wrong.

She picked up the lantern carefully and lowered it from the shelf in order to extinguish the flame. That was when a glint of silver caught her eye. There in the bottom of the tea light, under the now molten transparent wax lay a small silver key shimmering in the flickering candle light attached to the other end of the second white wick.

"The lady with the lamp." She smiled to herself. Figures why she always had her lamp with her, she thought.

Sam reached in, taking hold of the white wick, she gently pulled the key out of its waxy pool. She used the wax cloth to rub it clean, making sure not to touch the hot metal directly until it had cooled.

Once she had made her way back to the safe, she braced herself.

She slid the key into the safe's keyhole and turned it. Then with a satisfying clunk she twisted the handle and the safe door opened.

Inside, the first thing she noticed was two small vials of the luminous drug, safely inside a protective platinum case. She picked them up and placed them carefully in her pocket, praying that the cases were strong enough to keep them safe.

Also inside the safe was a folder. She picked it up and leafed through the contents. It contained numerous pages of chemical notation and formulas in Dr Henderson's distinct handwriting. She flipped through the pages until she got to a "Notes" section which she skimmed:

---

...The Subject has proved very gifted... a very strong fixation... motivated by a strong sexual desire... for the same sex...

---

She flipped on through the next few pages. The "Personal notes" section caught her eye.

---

...I find myself responding... unable to resist... I can only hope that I can remain objective long enough to find a different trigger—for both our sakes and the sake of the programme...

Sam took a deep breath and wiped away the errant tear that she was unable to hold back. Now was not the time for mourning. She had to try to make up for what she had done.

Sam suddenly became aware of voices echoing down the corridor and through the closed door into the office.

She pushed herself along the furniture and walls to the door. She opened the door a fraction to find out what was happening.

Through the crack she saw Director Morten at the gate insisting that he should be let through to see Dr Elms at once. Thankfully, it seemed Dr Elms had more clout with his fellow soldiers than Morten did and they were refusing him entry for the moment.

Sam knew she had to move quickly. She was not sure if Jesse would make it back to the office so she had to get out of there on her own, somehow.

She reluctantly stuffed Dr Henderson's notes and Jesse's employment records into the hearth. She glanced over at the lighter and the lantern still burning on the bookshelf on the far side of the office.

A further commotion at the gate drifted back through the crack in the door, causing her to change her mind and opt for the quickest solution. She retrieved one of the vials from her pocket and removed it from its platinum protective case. She stood as far back as she could from the hearth and flung the vial at the grate.

On impact it exploded into a ball of unnatural, luminous flames that rapidly consumed not only the contents of the grate in the hearth but, almost immediately, started to lick up the wall causing billows of smoke to rapidly fill the room and spill out into the corridor.

"Attention. Fire. Attention. Fire. Please evacuate," the electronic alarm sounded.

Immediately the automatic sprinkler system came on dowsing the room but not having much immediate effect on the fervent fire.

Sam took a deep breath and held it as she crawled along the floor back over to her wheelchair. She pulled herself up so that she was able to rest her upper body on the seat of the wheelchair. Using the wheelchair for support she propelled herself towards the door of the office. Once at the door she glanced at the gate. The smoke had begun to bellow out through the office door thick and fast.

Just then Lady Frost arrived at the gate. The two Timms wasted no time in unlocking the gate and allowing her through. Director Morten followed more hesitantly, not committing to the smoky corridor with as much gusto as Lady Frost.

Luckily, by then the smoke was pouring down the corridor and, Sam hoped, completely obscuring the door from the rest of the hallway. She gritted her teeth against the pain and fatigue and propelled herself out of the office, along the corridor, in the opposite direction away from the gate.

As soon as Lady Frost was clear of the gate she broke into

a run toward the smoking office. The soldiers had told her that Dr Elms and a patient were inside.

When she reached the door she crouched low and made her way inside. Finally she located Dr Elms sitting at the desk in the centre of the room. There was no sign of the patient. It could not be that hard to miss a wheelchair, could it?

A few minutes later Lady Frost emerged from the smoke, dragging Dr Elms.

"Quick, get the paramedics," she choked out, struggling to catch her breath. As soon as she had her breath back she started CPR on him.

---

For Sam, progress was slow. She needed the wheelchair for support but it was very awkward to manoeuvre, not to mention the thick smoke that followed her down the corridor made it very hard to see where she was going.

Sam had grown very tired and was hardly moving. She collapsed on the wheelchair, waiting. For what? She had no idea. All she knew was she was overcome with fatigue. Her world slowly went dark.

When she regained consciousness she noticed the smoke had dissipated somewhat. She was not sure how long she had been out cold but they must have managed to subdue the fire and started the smoke extraction.

When she looked around she found she was a few meters from a dead end in the form of an unmanned gate.

Sam licked her dry lips and chuckled sardonically to herself. What are the chances this gate would be open. Her heart sank. There weren't even soldiers guarding it that she could somehow convince or trick into letting her through like before.

She propelled herself up to the gate. From her position in the wheelchair she could not reach the handle. So she pushed herself off the chair and then leaning against the wall propelled herself into a half standing position. She braced herself and tried the handle, giving it a futile push, just to be sure. No such luck.

She glanced back in the direction of Dr Henderson's office, considering her options.

She could hear the commotion coming from that direction and she was pretty sure that the paramedics and emergency services would now be swarming that area. The soldiers would also most certainly be looking for the mystery patient that was taken to Dr Elms by now.

Tired, worn out, frustrated and aching all over, from the effects of the drug and the effort of fleeing, she leant back against the gate.

She was on the verge of accepting defeat.

After all, she had done what she could to make amends. At least she had prevented Dr Henderson's work from falling into the wrong hands. She was pretty certain that she was now in possession of the only vial of the drug in existence. She fingered the case in her pocket.

All she had to do was drop the last vial at her feet and her journey would end in a flash.

---

In a dark room, lit only by a black and white pixelated

monitor which showed Sam slumped, helpless, at the gate, a hand thumbed a small Lighthouse pendant.

The hand moved quickly to flip a switch.

The gate latch buzzed open.

The hand moved and placed the small Lighthouse pendant into a lab-coat pocket.

The buzz seemed to penetrate Sam's consciousness. She realised it was the latch. She mustered her strength, glancing up at the camera diagonally above her, thanking whoever was behind this miracle before she lunged at the gate, propelling herself and the wheelchair through it.

## 17

Jesse entered The Cage trying to look as purposeful as possible. He did not want his demeanour to draw attention to the fact he was not supposed to be there.

Inside he found Anthony very focussed on the monitors, dials, and readings produced by the twelve new Subjects left in his care. Two armed soldiers were keeping a close eye on him—not that the soldiers would be able to understand anything he was doing, Anthony thought.

Jesse felt for Anthony. Although he was probably the most laid back guy Jesse had ever known, his uncharacteristic erratic movements and nervous tic, of regularly tugging at his collar, showed he was feeling the pressure.

"Bit busy in here," Jesse said hoping to sound light hearted.

"Hmm," Anthony said without taking his eyes of the dials. "The big chief is off doing something more important."

"What could possibly be more important?" Jesse said, thinking of Elms sitting slumped at Dr Henderson's desk right now.

"Beats me, bro," Anthony said making a note on his clipboard.

Jesse had learnt enough, during his past few weeks of observing the trials on Sam, to know that the new Subjects were advancing through the various trials rather rapidly. He had a pretty good idea of what Dr Henderson would have thought about such recklessness. Each soldier was hooked up to a mask similar to the one Sam had been made to wear, before Dr Henderson came to the rescue. They were currently being subjected to rigorous Conditioned Behavioural Response therapy. Jesse thought back to when Anthony had explained to him what Dr Elms was doing.

This technique had its origins in Aversion Therapy as introduced in the 1950s. Each Subject had various predefined stimuli imposed on them and then they were either punished or rewarded, by either shocking or not shocking them accordingly and, so doing, building an appropriate response to each stimulus.

Jesse was on edge and needed to get back to Sam as soon as possible but he did not want to draw attention to himself. He resolved to try to hang about for a little while longer. He stood to one side and watched the soldiers. In an attempt to seem casual he stuck his hands in his pockets and was surprised to feel something hard in the bottom of his left hand pocket. He suddenly remembered the disk Anthony had dropped in the Lab.

This gave him an idea.

To the left of where he was standing stood a large control panel on wheels. After the observation room had burnt out and the military had taken over, a lot of new panels had been brought into the Cage. Seems the Military did not prioritise subjective observation enough to reinstate the Observation room and favoured more hands on approach. This panel, however, Jesse recognised as one that housed the disk player, which provided the input to the masks the Subjects were wearing.

When the two patrolling soldiers had their back turned to him, Jesse moved in closer to the disk player and swapped the disk in the player for the Erotic 01 disk and hit play.

Satisfied, Jesse casually moved away from the panel and watched for a few more minutes.

First one, then a second, then another and soon all twelve soldiers had developed erections, visible under the white sheets that covered them, where they lay on the gurneys.

He smiled to himself, pretty sure that this would mess up the data a bit and, hopefully, go a little way to setting back their progress. Who knows, he thought, it might teach you to make love not war, boys.

Just then one of the patrolling soldiers noticed a comrade's predicament.

For a brief tense moment Jesse thought he had been caught.

Then he saw the soldier glance around, more concerned about whether someone had noticed him noticing. When he found no one watching he obviously decided to turn a blind eye. Jesse assumed that he probably did not welcome the embarrassment or ragging he'd have to endure once the story spread through his Unit.

Jesse decided it was time to head back to Sam before anyone noticed anything amiss.

"Okay, since you seem to have it all under control here,

I'd better go find something useful to do. They're keeping me pretty busy with other stuff," Jesse said to Anthony.

"Yeah, laters, bro." Anthony did not look up from the file in which he was frantically scribbling notes.

---

When Jesse heard that there had been an incident in the Administration Wing he had feared the worst. He had tried his best to make his way back to Sam but the corridors were teeming with soldiers either on patrol or looking for someone. The latter made him feel hopeful. He hoped that it meant Sam was still alive and hopefully hiding somewhere safe in the facility.

He had to find her before they did.

A long while later, Jesse had searched every corridor still in operation in and around the Administration Wing but could not find Sam anywhere. He was beginning to worry that they had found her and taken her away while he had been wasting time scouring corridors in false hope.

He tried to put himself in Sam's position once again. If the roles were reversed and he was unable to make it out of the building on his own steam, where would he go?

It would have to be somewhere fairly close by, where the soldiers would not be able to easily find her.

Jesse suddenly realised that he had wandered into the corridor where he and Sam had first observed the first ADV Subjects in the little labs on their very first day on the ADV Program. Since the incident in The Cage, and the Military's involvement, all lab activity unrelated to the priority Subjects had been suspended leaving these labs on the corridors completely deserted.

Then it dawned on him. What better place to hide than in plain sight?

Jesse felt a bolt of renewed hope as he rushed from observation window to observation window.

Finally, there, he saw Sam's small frail figure slumped in the wheelchair inside one of the labs.

She had chosen well. The mini Lab she was in was on the border between the deserted area and the active wings which still housed some Subjects that were not ready to be released just yet.

How she had managed to get there from the Administration Wing he had no idea. She was slouched in the wheelchair, very still, and seemed unconscious. Fear gripped him and he hoped he was not too late.

He rushed over to her and felt for a pulse. It was very weak. She was hardly breathing. He had to act soon.

He rummaged around in the Mini Lab's cabinets until he found what he was looking for. He grabbed a syringe dispenser from the drawer, loaded it with the single Adrenaline dose and punched it into Sam's unconscious body. Using Adrenaline like this was only to be done in the case of an emergency.

If there ever was an emergency, this was it, he thought.

"Sam, can you hear me? Sam?" He waited, rubbing her hand.

Finally, Sam gasped and moaned as she came to.

It was only then that he noticed her body and clothes were wet through—probably from the fire sprinklers.

"Did you find the drug?" he asked gently.

Sam nodded very slightly.

He felt her forehead. "Jesus! You are burning up." He realised that half the sheen on her body must have been from perspiration. "We've got to get you out of here."

He thought he heard her say something. He leant in closer placing his ear as close to her mouth as possible.

"What about the others?" she breathed.

Jesse briefly glanced back in the direction of The Cage and allowed a small smirk to cross his lips.

"Oh, I think they'll be fine," he answered.

Sam opened her eyes, trying to understand what he meant.

"Let's just say they've just experienced an upturn in their army careers."

With new resolve to get Sam out in one piece, he grabbed the syringe dispenser and another dose of Adrenaline and slid them into his pocket before he grasped the back of the wheelchair and headed toward the main lobby. To get out of the building, they would need to pass by the Lab where they held Sam. It meant, passing the two guards on the door —an experience Jesse was not looking forward to.

As they rounded the corner, onto the corridor where the Lab was, Jesse saw the two guards animatedly talking to Lady Frost. They were gesticulating.

"Ah shit!" Jesse said under his breath. "It seems they have discovered you are gone." He made a quick decision and propelling the wheelchair straight ahead down another corridor perpendicular to the one the Lab was on. They would have to find another way to get to the main Lobby or wait until the guards had gone.

Jesse and Sam found themselves finally on a dark deserted corridor. Jesse, for one, was very relieved to be alone for a change. He used this opportunity to look over Sam quickly. It seemed the Adrenaline had had a positive effect and she was looking a lot more alert.

As they advanced farther down the corridor, Jesse was surprised to see a light coming through the vision-panel of a room at the far end of the corridor.

"I thought they'd closed this wing," he said trying to control his voice so that Sam could hear it but it would not echo too far down the empty corridor. He pushed Sam toward the light.

Jesse pulled up the wheelchair just outside the door where the light was coming from. He peeped in through the vision-panel. Before he could stop her Sam had pushed herself up and also peered into the room.

Sam recognised the room as the large gym where she and Jesse had first met, however now the room was almost completely empty with only a half dozen gurneys occupying the centre of the floor space.

Sam's breath caught. On five of those gurneys lay five small children. Three of them were girls of varying ages between three and nine and two boys Sam guessed were around six and eight. They were strapped to the gurneys and hooked up to mask headsets like the one used on her by Dr Elms.

Just then a soldier's head passed by the small vision-panel, causing them both to jump and duck instinctively.

"Those are children, not soldiers," Sam whispered.

"I don't understand," Jesse whispered back. "Isn't it illegal to involve children under eighteen in such trials?"

"That's probably why they are kept here in a disused corridor," Sam said. "We have to get them out."

Jesse could not believe his ears. It was hard enough smuggling Sam out the first time, let alone having to do it a second time, but the prospect of doing the same with five small children as well was just ludicrous.

"How?" he hissed in disbelief. However, he recognised the resolve in Sam's face and knew it was pointless to argue.

"We will need a diversion," he said. "Do you think you can do that thing you did with Elms on the corridor again?"

Sam shook her head. "It was only a silhouette. The only reason it worked was because you could not see him close up." She sat down back in the wheelchair, "And, I think the drug is wearing off."

They both knew that without the help of her projections it would be a lot harder to get out. She dropped her head into her hands.

Jesse grabbed hold of the wheelchair and wheeled her away from the door to the nearest abandoned lab where they could think without the immediate risk of being discovered by the soldiers guarding the children.

"We need a plan," he said.

Sam tried to think. Then she remembered. She stuck her hand in her pocket and brought out the last vial of the drug she had taken from Dr Henderson's safe.

"I thought you'd destroyed them," Jesse hoped she was not thinking what he was thinking.

"I haven't had a chance to yet," Sam said.

Jesse could see a twinkle in Sam's eye as the idea grew. He

was pretty sure he knew what she was thinking. He shook. "No way! Absolutely not!"

"Come on, Jess. We have no choice... I have no choice."

"Yes we do." Jesse thought quickly. "I know! I'll set a fire using the drug in one of these empty labs and the evacuation will hopefully provide enough cover and chaos to get you and the children out."

Sam grabbed his hand bringing his attention back to her. She shook her head. "One real fire is not going to be enough and if it is, it'll be too dangerous... I can't have someone else die... You have to inject me."

Jesse shook his head. "No. You're not strong enough. It'll kill you."

"Please," she said. "We have to get them out. There's no time. Let me do this. It's the only way."

Jesse knew deep down she was right. But he also knew the chances that she would survive another dose of the drug so soon, on top of her already depleted system, was very low.

Sam took the vial, removed it from its protective case and held it out to him as steadily as she could, trying not to show how scared she was.

Reluctantly he took the vial, searching her eyes for any sign that she wanted to change her mind. Instead, he noticed her clench her jaw and lift her chin in that determined manner he had seen so many times during the past few weeks, when she absolutely refused to fail.

He sighed and retrieved the syringe dispenser he had slipped into his pocket earlier and carefully loaded the drug vial.

She held out her arm, clamping her eyes shut.

He took a deep breath and punched the dispenser onto her skin injecting the drug into her vein.

As soon as the drug hit her system, Sam began to arch and convulse against the pain and sensory overload. She groaned and hissed as the hot fire of the liquid infused into her body. It was so excruciating! The blinding flashes of light, colour throbbing in her head and ears, feeling like cells were bursting, nerve endings searing.

Jesse watched in horror as her convulsions grew in magnitude until she arced like a bow.

Knowing that the drug was highly volatile and any rapid kinetic movement could cause it to auto combust, he tried to hold her down as best he could but without much success.

Suddenly he became aware of the noise she was making. The last thing they needed was for her to be heard and as a result for them to be discovered.

He let go of her and went to close the lab door.

When he turned back, she was completely quiet.

He panicked.

"Sam! Come on, Sam. Are you okay?" He reached for her pulse. It was back to almost non-existent. He was about to abort the idea of rescuing the children and just get her out of there when with a great whoosh a fire erupted in the lab on the other side of the corridor.

He looked down and saw Sam open her eyes a fraction and mouth the words, "Now, go."

## 18

Jesse stopped for a moment outside the lab where he had left Sam. He had made sure to position her in the shadows where she was not easy to spot. He had manoeuvred a modesty panel to help obscure her but sadly this was only partly possible.

Around him the fire had spread from the lab opposite all the way down the corridor. It looked so real!

He realised that it was not fooling the electronic safety systems and he needed to find a way to trigger the alarms. He remembered seeing an emergency button as they turned the corner into this deserted wing. He bolted through the fake flames over to it, slamming his palm down. Within a split second the electronic voice of the emergency alarm echoed through the corridor.

"Attention. Emergency. Attention. Emergency. Please evacuate."

Meanwhile, elsewhere in the building fires broke out, seemingly unprovoked. The empty gurney in Sam's original lab burst into flames. In The Cage the bank of instrument panels suddenly ignited. Within minutes the entire facility was in code blue evacuation mode.

Lady Frost stormed out of her office and into the main corridor to try to see what was causing the chaos.

"What the hell is going on?" she bellowed at one of her soldiers who was trotting past escorting a group of doctors out of the building.

When he saw her he immediately stood at attention. "Fires everywhere ma'am."

"Where is the girl? Find her!" she said.

"Yes, ma'am."

"And fast!"

"Yes, ma'am!" She trotted back in the opposite direction.

———

Jesse took a deep breath and hurled himself at the gym door propelling himself into the gym at speed. Instantly two rifles were pointed at him.

"Freeze!" barked one of the soldiers. He was a thick set, strawberry blond-haired guy with loads of freckles and a luscious ginger moustache.

Jesse's hands flew up into the air.

"I am! I am! I'm Orderly Jesse Wyatte. I've come from Dr Elms, I mean Sergeant Elms. He needs you in The Cage, on the double." Jesse spoke quickly.

"So what about these?" The blond soldier nodded at the children.

"I don't know," Jesse said. "All I know is Sergeant Elms is on a short fuse and there are fires everywhere."

Jesse saw the blond soldier look over his shoulder at the

other soldier behind him, whom Jesse had not had a chance to get a good look at yet. To his relief they seemed to believe him.

"But you're coming with us," the blond soldier barked as he grabbed Jesse by the shoulder. "Move!"

"I swear, come see for yourself," Jesse said. "I just want to get the hell out of here. Please, let me go. I'll do anything but I just do not want to burn to death like that doctor." It was not hard to sound genuine. He really did want to get out of there and did not want to burn alive, which he knew was also a possibility if Sam did not manage to control her movements.

Outside the gym, most of the corridor extending in Sam's direction was now fully ablaze, effectively preventing anyone from venturing down there. The only route open to them was leading away out to the main corridor in the direction of the lobby.

Good thinking, Sam, Jesse thought.

The sight of the flames seemed to convince the guards enough that Jesse was telling them the truth.

"Okay. Get out of here," one of them barked at Jesse, shoving him towards the door.

Jesse rushed on towards the main corridor to join the streams of staff and soldiers heading to the main exit to evacuate the facility. He was pleased that the two soldiers turned up stream and were obviously following orders to head to The Cage. Jesse kept going with the flow of rushing people, occasionally glancing back, until he could no longer see the two soldiers. Then he doubled back.

Once back on the deserted corridor Jesse saw that the fire was holding a steady pattern. He glanced in the direction of the lab where Sam was but resisted the urge to go check on her. He had to get the children out first.

In the gym he hurriedly switched off the headsets and untied the children and got them to sit up.

"You okay?" He gave them a quick examination to see that they were not hurt and were able to walk. They were a little bewildered and quite exhausted but otherwise, thankfully, they were in pretty good shape. "You guys have to come with me, okay?"

He grabbed a blanket and put it over his shoulders like a scarf. He then addressed the two oldest children, a girl who was around nine and the boy a little younger.

"I want you two to grab hold of these," he indicated the tail ends of the blanket "and hold hands with one of the little ones each, and do not let go of either, okay?"

He saw that they did as they were told and then he grabbed the last little girl. She was around three, but very small and frail. He grabbed another blanket, wrapped it around her then popped her on his hip.

"Ready?" he asked.

They nodded.

"Okay. Hold on now and no matter what happens do not let go."

They headed for the door.

Jesse escorted them down the corridor and into the main drag to the lobby. He shielded them and corralled them to the main entrance and finally up and out to the surface.

Above-ground a number of fire engines and ambulances had already gathered. It was chaos. Panicked people were pouring out of every emergency exit.

Jesse picked his way through the crowds choosing gaps in the sea of bodies where it was easier for the children to run alongside him.

Finally, not far ahead of him, he saw a single ambulance standing almost on its own. Jesse headed for it. The children were soaked and, after everything they had been through, he was keen for them to be placed in good hands and checked over properly. He also hoped that the paramedics would be more interested in the children's health than in asking him a lot of questions about where they had come from.

As he neared the ambulance he saw an older, buxom woman sitting on the step of the ambulance with a thick blanket around her shoulders. It was Margery.

Sensing someone approaching she looked up and saw them. Her jaw dropped.

"Children? I didn't realise we had children here." Without waiting for a response, Margery reached out and grabbed the little one from Jesse's hip and enveloped her in a motherly hug before she corralled the other four around her. "Oh what little darlings!" she crooned.

"Please can you have them checked over by the paramedics?" Jesse said. "I have to go back."

Jesse considered what else to tell her but it was obvious that no explanation was necessary. She was only concerned that they be looked after.

Jesse thanked his lucky stars and headed back up stream towards the facility.

Jesse ran down the corridor to the lab where he had left Sam. He had to be very careful navigating the flames because, as he soon realised, even though these flames were technically an illusion, his mind had difficulty distinguishing them from real flames. It seemed the illusion was powerful enough to cause his autonomous nervous system to believe he was actually feeling the heat and cause his skin to react as if he was actually being burnt.

Finally he reached Sam's side. She looked terrible. She was sweating profusely, her eyes were still closed.

"Sam, can you hear me? Sam?" Her pulse was even weaker than before. "I know you are still in there. Sam, can you hear me? We've got to get you out of here, now."

Sam could feel the hands on her shoulders and had a sense someone was talking to her, but she could not hear what they were saying over the roar of fire in her ears. She used all her will power to force her eyes to open a little, but all she could make out was a form of a person bent over her, flames all around.

She felt herself being dragged, dragged to safety. She had to know. "Did we save them?" she croaked.

"Yes," the voice of her saviour reached her ears. "They're safe."

"Good," she whispered. She could not leave them to die in that shed.

She lost consciousness.

## 19

It had been six months since Sam's narrow escape from PhyCorp.

The code blue evacuation had caused enough chaos to give Jesse sufficient cover to smuggle Sam out of the facility. Once outside it was easy enough to enlist the help of a paramedic to get Sam in an ambulance and head to the hospital. Once at the hospital Jesse knew he would need to be creative to get Sam away from the Emergency room. If the doctors took a closer look at Sam they would know something was terribly wrong and the chances were that she would end up back at PhyCorp before he could even say fake fire.

However, once at the hospital, he was relieved to find that there was enough chaos and mayhem to allow them to slip away.

Jesse hoped that the Military would not be out looking for them. He hoped by destroying his employee records he had sufficiently covered his tracks to prevent them tracing Sam back to him. He also knew that PhyCorp had an official anonymity policy for all their Subjects, making sure that they collected as little personal data about their Subjects as possible. Whether this was genuine, or just a ruse to allow people to come forward and volunteer more willingly, he was less sure of. Then there was also the question about Sam, their star Subject, and whether the same rules of anonymity were extended to her.

Not wanting to risk getting caught at his home, Jesse called in a favour with an old friend, Michelle, who lived a couple of miles away from the hospital. She was mostly away working in the big city. She had lent him her apartment a couple of times before, when he needed some space from his housemates, or on the one occasion she convinced him he needed to entertain a girl. Her apartment was not smart or posh, but it was clean and central, which meant he could get food and medical supplies from the hospital when he needed until he had nursed Sam back to health.

It took Sam about a month to regain most of her strength after which she soon began to feel edgy and cooped up in the tiny apartment. She wanted to go home, to her little cottage on the edge of the sea. She needed the isolation and its safe sanctuary.

Jesse, however, thought that was a very bad idea and tried to convince her to consider relocating somewhere new where the Military could not find her.

Sam was not swayed easily. She was sure she had not given PhyCorp, or any of its staff, any information about her home village or any other personal details and thus it would be perfectly safe to go home.

Jesse could not argue with the fact that he was the closest

person to her and even he did not know her second name or anything else about her.

Conversely, in their time together, he had become an open book and happily shared oodles of details about himself and his family with Sam. He had no family left after they had all either died in the War Zone or from poor health due to a lack of medical supplies available to civilians. After their death he had given up the modest family home on the West coast in order to start a new life somewhere else, thus giving him ties to nowhere.

So, it did not take much persuasion to convince Jesse to return to her village and start a new life for himself there too. Besides, after everything they had been through together, he was now like a little brother to her and she was the closest he would get to a sister.

Sam's welcome back to The Lighthouse Pub was, somewhat characteristically, unconventional.

Sam had travelled dressed as a man in Jesse's clothes, complete with a hat and scarf to avoid being identified, in the event the Military were still looking for her. She walked into the pub and before removing her hat and scarf ordered Jesse and herself a pint from Megs who was serving. Whether because she was so well disguised or because Sam was the last person Megs was expecting to turn up at the pub, Megs did not recognise her. It was only once Megs had poured them a pint and was standing awaiting payment that Sam took off her hat and scarf.

"Hello, Megs," she said softly.

Megs stood in front of her without moving for a long moment. Then a swift right palm connected squarely with Sam's left cheek, making almost the entire clientele in the pub flinch in sympathy.

Sam stood there, unflinching, gritting her teeth at the pain. "I deserve that," she said simply.

Their eyes met and Megs crumbled. She rushed out from behind the bar and threw her arms about Sam.

"I was so worried I had lost you!" Megs cried on Sam's shoulder.

Megs had heard about the incident at PhyCorp.

"After hearing all the stories from Mr Bow I was sure you were dead and that I would never see you again."

"I am sorry," Sam said. "I did not mean to make you worry. I am fine."

Megs dried her tears. "No I am sorry. Nothing is worth losing family over. I am sorry I said what I did."

Sam hugged Megs tightly. "I am sorry I did what I did."

At that moment Pete walked in.

Sam grew rigid. She did not know what to expect.

Megs noticed what she was looking at.

"Sam, we have some news," Megs said as she held out her hand towards Pete. He came closer taking her hand.

Megs brought her hand, now holding Pete's closer to Sam.

That is when Sam saw the tiny little rings on each of their fingers. She looked up at Megs who was now smiling, and Pete too.

"We are getting married in the spring," Megs admitted looking at Pete lovingly.

Sam was thrilled for them. She hugged them both.

When she finally let go, and stood back, Megs continued, "and," she patted her stomach, "you will be an auntie a few months after."

Sam embraced her in another enthusiastic hug realising, a little too late, that she needed to be gentler with her sister now that she was pregnant.

"Well, in that case you are going to need all the help you can get and I happen to know someone who would be very keen to help you out in the pub." Sam stepped back making space for Jesse in the conversation. "Meet my close friend, Jesse Wyatte."

Megs and Pete welcomed Jesse and few days later he began his new life as the Lighthouse Pub bar manager, a role he seemed to enjoy thoroughly.

Sam had decided to go back to writing, which was where it all started. It was due to her skill and success as a young journalist, before the war, that she was selected for active duty to accompany the troops and report on the war effort from the front line.

At first, this was a highly exhilarating prospect and one she had accepted eagerly. She had never supported taking up arms as a way to resolve conflict, but she liked the idea of being able to report and bring the truth to the world back home. However, it was not long after she had arrived at the Front that she realised that there was no such thing as a truth she could share.

No matter which way she told any story, there was always a different perspective, and more often than not a loaded one, sometimes more powerful and more damaging than the loaded barrel of a gun.

That was why she had now decided to turn her hand to fiction. She wanted to harness the power of words and ideas to inspire dreams and ideologies that transcended the current restrictive, prohibitive world around them. She believed that only once people were inspired, and started to dream or think differently, could they truly start to change their reality. So, she started The Lighthouse Chronicles, a regular little subversive gazette that told stories of men and women who fought the brave fight to make their world a better place. Despite intending it to be a work of fiction, she found that a lot of inspiration for her articles and stories came from real life acts of courage and bravery.

Sam sat at a table near the window in the conservatory of her cottage, overlooking the bay. She stared at her laptop. A blank page stared back at her. For some reason she was struggling to get into the flow of writing. She tugged at her now spiky hair in frustration. She really wished she could concentrate.

The doorbell rang.

She groaned and tried to ignore it.

It rang again.

She grumbled as she got up and headed to the front door, shouting before she even got there. "Megs, I said I'll come up for dinner later. I don't need..."

She threw the door open expecting Megs to be standing on her doorstep with a hearty, homemade lunch. However, standing in front of her, on the small rubber doormat, was a person she thought she would never see again, Dr Victoria Henderson.

There was a long, motionless pause as Sam tried to process this new information. The more she tried to comprehend how it was possible the more her mind drew a blank, exacerbated by the growing red mist that crept across her vision.

"Hi," Victoria said swallowing the lump in her throat. She knew this moment was not going to be easy. Even so, she had persisted for three months, after the chaos at the institute had died down, to try to find Sam. She was not going to back down now. "Someone at the Lighthouse Pub said I'd find you here."

Without so much as a twitch of a muscle Sam stared at Victoria.

Victoria's resolve started to crack under the tension and she glanced around as if looking for something to give her strength to keep going.

"Do you mind if I come in?" she finally asked, rubbing her arms against the seaside chill.

## 20

On the day of the explosion, Victoria just about had time to grab the three vials before she realised the chemicals in the Cage were going to blow.

To the right of the Cage she saw an emergency exit. She, thankfully, had the forethought to make sure that at least all the emergency protocols had been strictly adhered to in the construction of the Cage, including the installation of at least two emergency exits on either side in addition to the main doors.

She bolted for the nearest one and only made it in the nick of time. The explosion flung her half way down the little corridor, which ran along the side of the hall, and rendered her unconscious.

When she came to, Jim, the surveillance guard was hovering over her. Luckily, he had noticed her lying in that narrow little corridor. If no one had found her she would most certainly have died.

Unluckily, he notified Morten of her predicament before she could regain consciousness.

Morten feared Victoria would report him to the board, and the military, for not exercising due care and pushing the project's timelines beyond what was sensible and prudent, thereby risking the lives of the staff and Subjects, as well as placing the entire institute and their research at risk. So, when he discovered what had happened, he saw this as a perfect opportunity to rescue this situation in his favour. He had her whisked away and locked up in Jim's surveillance room, allowing everyone to believe she had died in the fire.

She was pretty sure he would use the information he had gathered about her past to smear her name and reputation, claiming it provided justification for why she would have acted so irresponsibly and attempted such a dangerous and irrational experiment in the first place.

While she was being held hostage in the little dark surveillance room, she had the excruciating experience of having to watch Sam's progress while feeling utterly helpless and frustrated by her incarceration.

So, when she saw Sam cornered at the gate at the opposite end of the Administration block, she had to act. Thankfully, Jim was transfixed by another bank of monitors on the other side of the room, distracted by the commotion created by the fire and smoke in her office. This was her chance. She seized the opportunity to help Sam and flicked the switch to let Sam free.

She hoped that at least that would give Sam a chance to escape.

## 21

Lady Frost, in her turquoise suit sat behind Morten's old desk, reading the incriminating file he had on Dr Henderson. On the desk lay the USB stick.

Dr Henderson knocked on the door. "You wanted to see me, General."

"Ah, Dr Henderson. Please come in and take a seat," Lady Frost said.

Victoria noticed the file Lady Frost had open before her. Instantly her heart felt heavy. She took a deep breath, bracing herself for the inevitable. She expected two soldiers to arrive at the office door any second to take her away like they had Martin.

At least Lady Frost had the integrity to call her to her office and so avoid the humiliation of being dragged away in front of her colleagues.

Victoria slowly walked over to the chair and took a seat in front of the desk.

"I found this in Morten's things," Lady Frost began. She glanced through the open pages one more time before she closed the file and dropped it on the table in front of Victoria. "I assume you knew he had it?"

Victoria dropped her eyes and nodded.

Lady Frost took a deep breath, got up and headed to the decanter. "Care for a drink?" she asked.

Victoria shook her head. She needed this to be over quickly.

"Sometimes the foolish actions of a single man can undermine an entire nation," Lady Frost said while she poured a finger of Scotch into a crystal tumbler. She took a large sip and returned to her position behind her desk. "I am sorry." She paused. "We thought we were backing the right man." She put her glass down and slid over a cheque, which Victoria had not noticed before, that had been lying to one side on the desk.

Victoria did not look at it, choosing to keep a watchful eye on Lady Frost's face to understand where this conversation was heading.

"What is that for?" she asked.

"It's to help you start again."

"General, with all due respect I cannot work for the Military."

Lady Frost nodded her head as if she knew that would be Victoria's response. "I respect that." She paused for a moment. "But everything is not always what it seems, Dr Henderson... I'm not only military."

"As a scientist I need to remain impartial and independent," Victoria said.

"And that, I hope, is exactly what you'll be."

Victoria felt confused. Somehow, she got the feeling the tables had turned without her knowledge. She decided to cut to the chase. "What is it you want in return then?" she asked.

"That you do what you are good at," Lady Frost said with a slight smile.

Victoria could not help the sardonic chuckle that escaped her lips. "Nothing more?" She waited briefly for a reply. When none came she shook her head. "I can hardly believe that. We both know that, where large sums of money are concerned, there are always conditions or strings attached."

Lady Frost smiled and nodded in understanding. She held Victoria's gaze.

"What, really? No strings?" Victoria asked.

Lady Frost merely help her gaze.

"Not even regular reports on how I spend the money?" Victoria pressed. This was surreal.

"No. In fact, the one thing I do ask—"

"I knew it—"

Lady Frost gave her a warning look.

"...is that you keep it top secret and tell us as little as possible. This is all based on trust, Victoria."

"And you trust me?" Victoria could not read Lady Frost.

Lady Frost nodded.

Victoria suddenly caught sight of the file on her on Lady Frost's desk. "Oh, I get it. You know you can trust me because you have the right leverage."

"Victoria, I assume your evident cynicism is one of the characteristics that make you such a good scientist." Lady Frost picked up the file.

Victoria swallowed, waiting for the guillotine to fall.

Instead Lady Frost sauntered over to the burning hearth behind where Victoria sat.

Victoria watched her intently. She could not hold out any longer.

"What are you going to do with that?"

Lady Frost did not reply. She opened the file and glanced at the contents again. "I understand this is ancient history?"

Victoria nodded, her throat dry.

Lady Frost closed the folder and held it over the fire. "Well, then unless you want to keep it as a souvenir..." She met Victoria's gaze questioningly.

Victoria shook her head, still not able to bring herself to speak.

Lady Frost dropped the folder into the fire and watched it catch alight and begin to burn, the photo paper melting and colouring in the flames.

Without turning back to Victoria Lady Frost said, "So, if you are willing to accept my word, unless there is something else you feel you would like to discuss, you are free to go."

A stunned Victoria got up, hesitating briefly before she picked up the cheque, still not looking at it. She turned back toward Lady Frost. "Who are you?"

Lady Frost smiled into the fire but did not answer.

Victoria nodded to herself, understanding the silent response, and headed to the door.

"Oh, Victoria," Lady Frost stopped her before she got to the door. "Good luck with finding her. If you do, tell her—" she hesitated for a moment before she shook her head, "never mind."

Victoria turned and left.

Sam finally willed her feet into action and she backed away from the door, rapidly retreating into the cottage.

Victoria took that as an invitation and stepped inside, closing the door behind her. Her attention was instantly drawn to the exquisite view of the bay and the distant lighthouse, through large floor-to-ceiling windows, on the far side of the room. She looked around and took in the large living-dining room with its high beamed ceiling.

On the left, nearest to her position was a small six-seater wooden dining room table and chairs. Beyond that, on the left of the room, stood a welcoming fireplace surrounded by two comfortable couches, one positioned facing the fireplace, the other looking towards the awesome view.

On the right, opposite the fireplace, stood a prominent marble topped island counter in front of a modest kitchen area.

"Nice place," she ventured, aware of how unsure her voice sounded.

Sam had headed straight for the kitchen and was pouring

herself a glass of water, which she sipped thirstily hoping the cool liquid would somehow calm the turbulent emotions boiling in her gut. She remained like that facing the sink, sipping the water.

Victoria advanced farther into the space feeling drawn in by the view and needing closer proximity to Sam.

"Wow! What a great vie—"

Sam slammed down the glass of water and turned to face Victoria. "You've got a nerve!" Her voice was breathy and thick with venom.

Victoria instantly turned her attention to Sam. Having advanced to beyond the island counter she slowly approached it, and Sam.

"Look Sam, I'm sorry—"

"Pitching up here like this, six months later as if nothing has happened."

"It was not easy finding you!"

"How did you—" A chilling vice like grip seized her chest as suspicions that the Military had been tracing her movements flooded her mind, "…find me?"

Victoria dipped her hand into her pocket and pulled out the Lighthouse pendant. She reached forward and held it out to Sam. When Sam did not take it, she gently lowered it onto the marble counter between them.

Sam watched the movement in silence and then turned away abruptly, leaning on the sink with both hands for support.

Victoria instinctively needed to reach out to Sam and approached her cautiously around the counter. When she got close enough, she gingerly stretched out her hand and touched Sam's shoulder, needing to make contact.

The moment Sam felt the soft hesitant touch something inside snapped. She turned abruptly and grabbed the outstretched hand, tears rimming her eyes. "You made me think you were dead!"

Victoria searched Sam's eyes, holding her gaze as she slowly and with measured steps moved toward her. It felt like she was approaching a wild animal, afraid that any rapid actions would scare her prey. Finally, only inches apart, Victoria leaned in and tentatively planted a soft kiss on Sam's lips. When Sam let it happen, closing her eyes as if entranced, Victoria followed up with a few more soft pecks on her lips.

She pulled away slightly and continued feather light kisses on Sam's jaw-line and neck.

Sam leant her head to the side giving Victoria more access, lost in the moment.

Suddenly, Sam snapped out of her stupor. She grabbed Victoria by the upper arms and shoved her into the island counter behind her, causing a sensual gasp, due to the force of the impact, to escape her lips.

"You made me believe I fucking killed you!" Sam's rage, her voice laced with newly ignited arousal that was now bubbling dangerously close to the surface.

On seeing the unmistakable desire reflecting back at her in Victoria's eyes she pushed forward and enacted her punishment by devouring Victoria's lips roughly, almost violently.

When she pulled away, Victoria whimpered at the loss. "Please. I'll tell you everything."

When Sam did not pull away, Victoria lifted her hand and placed it on Sam's chest, running her fingers gently down from her collarbone towards her now pert nipples, straining against the fabric of her shirt.

Sam closed her eyes and pulled away slightly from the delicious assault.

Victoria leaned in and once again kissed her jaw-line, down her neck and between kisses whispered, "Just... Please...." There was a long silence as Victoria sucked on Sam's pulse point and then bit down gently, eliciting a groan from Sam.

Her anger only momentarily dowsed, Sam realised Victoria had stopped talking. She wanted to know. She once again shoved Victoria back into the counter to get her attention. "Please, what?"

Victoria looked up at her, a new fire burning behind hooded eyelids and her breath ragged. "Please," she breathed, "fuck me."

That was the spark to Sam's powder keg. She could not contain it any longer. She ripped Victoria's trousers open and shoved her hand down into her panties, surprised by how wet Victoria was.

"Oh God!" Victoria breathed as she dropped her head forward on Sam's shoulder and gripped her at the exquisite touch.

"Is this what you came here for?" Sam hissed, her anger mixing dangerously with her desire.

"No."

"Then what?" Sam asked, not letting up on her caresses of the soft smooth folds of Victoria's core. "Hmm? What did you come for?"

"To tell you..." Victoria was struggling to control her breathing, "what happened." Victoria threw her head back gasping.

Sam leaned forward and claimed her mouth in a powerful, passionate kiss, until they were forced apart by the desperate need for oxygen.

"Speak," she hissed, "or I'll stop."

"No! Please... Don't stop."

Victoria had the overwhelming desire to feel and touch Sam. She tried to unzip Sam's jeans but Sam effortlessly batted her hand away.

"Tell me," Sam demanded.

Victoria gritted her teeth and tried for her zipper again. This time she succeeded and slid her hand into Sam's jeans.

Sam groaned and bit her lip hard at the sensation of Victoria's cool fingers between her own, very wet, folds.

"Tell me or this is over." Sam slowed her caresses.

Victoria faintly nodded and swallowed. "The fire was an accident..."

Sam shook her head to focus. She was struggling not to be distracted by the incredible sensations of Victoria's fingers tentatively exploring her sex. "I now know that... the drugs caused it."

Victoria's breath caught as Sam slid two fingers into her core and started to take her. She forced herself to keep talking. "Morten and Elms were behind it!"

"Behind what?"

"Morten blackmailed me... into using the drugs on you."

"With what?" Sam's voice was just as ragged.

"The fact that I'm a dyke..." Victoria slid two fingers, then three into Sam's core eliciting a guttural moan from both of them. "And that I... Oh God...! Wanted... you." She began to pump into Sam matching the rhythmic motions of Sam's fingers filling her.

"How?" Sam asked.

"He had pictures."

"Of what?"

"Of me... and other women... Of you... and me."

Sam was finding it hard to fight the exquisite tension building up in her core and remain focussed.

"From when?"

"Your subconscious... gave us away.... Your dreams..."

Sam slid her thumb over Victoria's clit.

"Oh fuck!" Victoria bit her bottom lip, straining for more contact.

"The children?" Sam pushed, unable to string longer sentences together.

"Morten." Victoria's head fell back.

They were both now teetering dangerously close to the edge of orgasm, but Sam needed to know. She slowed her movements and lessened the pressure where Victoria needed it most.

"Oh God!... Please..." Victoria pleaded.

"Not the military?" she asked.

"No... But using Military funding."

"And Morten now?"

"Been Reset."

"And you?"

Sam re-engaged her thumb's caress of Victoria's clit, redoubling the thrusting motion of her fingers against Victoria's sensitive flesh causing her breath to catch, her head to roll back in a silent scream.

"I came... for you," Victoria finally forced out her words.

With that they both came together, violently.

———

They stood like that, collapsed into each other's frames, without moving, without retreating, without saying a word, just holding each other upright for a long while after they had finally ridden out the aftershocks.

"That was the smoothest interrogation technique I have ever seen." Victoria finally broke the silence once she had recovered enough to speak. "Did they teach you that in the army?"

Sam smiled against her shoulder. "You'd be surprised what they teach you in the Forces." Sam turned to look at the woman in her arms.

"Clearly you don't play fair," Victoria said.

"Nothing is ever fair in love or war." Sam smiled and looked deeply into Victoria's eyes before she planted a soft kiss on her nose.

"Well, in that case," Victoria said, "I have a lot to learn." She took Sam's hand and gently pulled her in the direction of the only door leading off from the large living-room. "I assume the bedroom is this way?"

"You are a quick study Dr Henderson," Sam said, allowing Victoria to lead her.

"So my teachers have always told me," Victoria said with a mischievous glint in her eye.

# EPILOGUE

It was a calm, sunny spring day and Sam was sitting in her usual writing place at the small table in the conservatory. Victoria appeared carrying two cups. She kissed Sam affectionately on the crown of her head as she placed the cup of coffee on the table next to Sam.

Sam, without looking away from the screen reached round and slipped her hand up the back under Victoria's top, rubbing her fingers gently over smooth skin.

Victoria remained there for a few long moments, relishing the caress, before she took her tea and headed to the soft wicker two-seater couch a few feet away facing out over the bay. She sat down, drew her feet up under her and sipped her herbal tea.

"So, I need to start looking for a place to set up my lab," she said conversationally.

Sam looked up briefly, only half-distracted from her writing task. "Oh? What were you thinking?" she asked.

Victoria tucked the folds of her summer dress around her knees and ankles. "Well, it has to be nearby, but secluded enough to be discreet, defensible and discourage casual and other interlopers. Ideally it should also be somewhere sort of symbolic but functional."

Sam finally looked away from the screen turning her attention to Victoria. "Oh. You mean like a secret lair?" Sam said teasingly.

Victoria blushed and they laughed. "Yes, maybe a bit. Ridiculous as it may sound," Victoria admitted.

"Oh, I don't know," Sam said. "I think every scientist needs a secret lair. Who knows, it might be easier than you think." Sam waggled her eyebrows again at Victoria.

"Yes, yes. I know I know... 'You don't know until you try,'" she quoted Sam. She picked up a cushion from the couch and threw it at Sam playfully.

Once the laughter had subsided Victoria put her cup down, sat back on the couch and admired the view.

Sam noticed she was worrying at the pinkie of her left hand.

"What's with you?" she asked mimicking Victoria's actions with her pinkie.

"Oh nothing." Victoria dismissed the action. Seeing that Sam was not buying it she studied the top of her left hand. "It's my ring. I think I finally lost it for good."

"Have you checked the sewers?" Sam teased.

"No. You're better at that than I am," Victoria said.

With that comment Sam got up from her chair and headed over to the couch sporting a mischievous smile and a raised eyebrow. "Really? Really?" She tackled Victoria, pinning her down on the couch and tickling her mercilessly. "What are you saying? That I do all your wet work and you are just the brains around here?"

Victoria let out a squeal of laughter. "A good team, I'd say," she offered as her defence.

Sam laughed happily, her heart filled with love for the beautiful woman beneath her.

A few days later Sam took Victoria out on Pete's boat. She told her she had an idea for her secret lair but that it was so top secret that she had to be blind-folded to be taken there.

Naturally, Victoria protested the entire way, citing all the logical reasons why she would have to know where it was. Eventually, she settled for pouting most adorably when Sam insisted that she play by the rules or the excursion was over.

After taking Victoria on a few wild detours to make sure she could not guess where they were headed, she moored the boat at the little jetty below her Grandmother's bequest—the Lighthouse that stood vigil at the edge of the bay.

Sam helped Victoria out of the boat and led her, still blindfolded, into the Lighthouse, up its spiral staircase and up to the top platform that ran around the lantern. Here she positioned Victoria so that she faced the vista looking out over the sea towards the land and, after gently kissing her shoulder in thanks for humouring her, undid the blindfold.

Victoria blinked for a few seconds, her eyes trying to adjust to having to work again. Suddenly her breath hitched. The view was exquisite. The dark-blue sea's mysterious expanse leading up to the four miles of golden sand that formed the edge of the bay. At first Victoria did not recognise the site, not until she saw the small clusters of houses, including a lone cottage, dotting the hillside.

"This is awesome," Victoria said. "I could never have imagined what the coast looked like from here."

"Fitting don't you think?" Sam asked.

Victoria glanced back confused.

"That our very own secret lair gives us a new perspective on things."

Victoria turned back and threw her arms around Sam's neck and kissed her deeply. She loved and appreciated this woman in her arms for her strength, her stamina, all her talents but also her thoughtfulness and care.

When the kiss ended Sam suddenly remembered something and dug around in her jacket pocket. "Oh, I almost forgot."

Victoria looked on intrigued.

Sam brought out a small ring box and handed it to Victoria, "I got you something."

Sam watched as Victoria took the box and unwrapped it. When she opened it her face lit up with delight.

"Oh my goodness." Victoria whispered at the sight of the small silver pinkie signature ring that sat snugly in the padded little box. It was engraved with a simple angled cube shape with three symmetrical lines, rays of light, extending outward on each side. Victoria instantly understood the allusions to a lantern, the light of the Lighthouse and even the first cube shape she got Sam to project on the screens in the Lab.

"Every scientist worth their salt needs to have a signature, don't you think?" Sam teased.

Victoria turned the ring over to find the small letters of an elegant engraving on the inside. She read it out aloud: "Man of Action."

"Since I wrecked your office and everything in it..." Sam said leaving the rest unspoken.

"It is beautiful, thank you." Victoria slid the ring on her finger and then threw her arms around Sam and kissed her passionately.

---

It had been a late start that day. It was well after midday and Victoria and Sam were still in bed, making love and dozing, intertwined in the sheets, not sure where one body ended and the next one began.

Finally after spending a few long moments watching the sleeping figure in her arms, Sam kissed her gently on her nose and got up out of bed. She was in her usual briefs and white vest top.

"Where are you going?" Victoria's groggy voice echoed softly.

"I think it is time I help this scientist to get cracking on setting up her lair today," Sam teased as she headed over to the washstand and poured water into the basin.

She rinsed her face, grabbed the small towel next to the basin and dried off. When she opened her eyes Victoria, in her long white sleep shirt, was standing behind her. Sam smiled at her raising an eyebrow expectantly, wanting to know what Victoria wanted.

Victoria wrapped her arms around Sam and spoke into the mirror as if it was the continuation of a conversation they had just been having. "And every scientist needs a front woman."

Victoria then pulled Sam around by the hips and released

a chain from her fist, using two hands to hold it up like she was awarding a medal.

Sam bowed her head in acceptance.

"What's this?" Sam examined the silver dog-tags hanging from the chain. On closer inspection she saw that the dog-tags were engraved with the same lantern symbol that was on Victoria's ring. She flipped it over and on the back it had the same, "Man of Action" neatly engraved.

"Will you be my superhero?" Victoria asked softly.

Sam raised an eyebrow. "That depends... Do you get to experiment on me again?"

Victoria laughed softly. "That's what scientists do."

Sam leaned forward and kissed Victoria deeply, soothing away all prospects of any real worries or concerns Victoria might have had about how Sam really felt about their time at the institute.

Sam finally pulled away and searched Victoria's eyes. "Yes, of course, it'll be an honour to be your superhero."

Somewhere else in the cottage a door closed.

"Hello. Where are you? Are you two decent?" Jesse's voice echoed through from the living room.

Punctuating her words with light kisses to Victoria's nose she said, "Of course... every superhero... also needs a Robin." She wiggled her eyebrows and cocked her head toward the sounds coming from the living room.

"In fact they need a team... of allies," Victoria added.

Jesse appeared at the door. Once he saw them in their partial state of undress he covered his eyes melodramatically and turned away. "Jesus, you two! Enough with the flesh already! It is almost midday. Can you please get decent? Megs sent me round with your lunch."

Sam and Victoria laughed and unhooked themselves. Victoria headed to the shower.

"What, Jess, you telling me you have not seen it all before as my P.C.A.?" Sam teased.

"That was different you were... just an..." he searched for the word "object."

Sam grabbed the towel from the side of the basin and, playfully brandishing it as a whip, she chased him back into the living room.

Back at the institute, Lady Frost sat behind her desk deep in concentration, trying to work through the new plans for the institute, when Margery knocked at the door.

"This came for you, ma'am." She entered the room and swiftly deposited a small brown package on Lady Frost's desk.

Lady Frost nodded. "Thanks Margery, I could have collected it from reception on my rounds."

"That's okay, ma'am. I figured it was important."

Lady Frost picked up the package and opened it. She studied the small ring in its snug little box. "Oh, it is, Margery," she said as she slid the ring on her pinkie finger. "It's very important."

## IF YOU ENJOYED THIS BOOK...

Reviews are one of the most important ways for me to gain visibility and bring my books to the attention of other readers.

If you've enjoyed this book, I would be very grateful if you could spend just five minutes leaving a review on your favourite reader platforms (it can be as short as you like).

It really can make a huge difference.

**Jump to your favourite reader platform now >>**

Alternatively, send me feedback here:

mail@SamSkyborne.com

Thank you very much!

## ACKNOWLEDGEMENTS

Thank you to my diligent Editorial, Production and Street Teams for your time, effort and careful consideration which helped me make this the best book it could be.

Thank you to all my wonderful family and friends who have lovingly and tirelessly helped and supported me on this journey. I love and thank you from the bottom of my heart!

Lastly, thank you to all my loyal readers. Your interest in and enjoyment of my stories is what makes it all worthwhile.

# WHY NOT TRY...

http://SamSkyborne.com/RISK/

"**RISK: Three Crime-fighting Women Risk All for Love, Lust &
Justice.**"

## ALSO BY SAM SKYBORNE

### Novels:

Simulation: The Dawn of a Superhero

RISK: Three Crime-fighting Women Risk All for Love, Lust and Justice

Alice

### Box Sets

Super Starter Box Set

### Lesbian Erotic Shorts (L.E.S) Story & Film:

Cat Sitting: Lesbian Cat Custody Complications

Saying Sorry: A Queer & Complex Process

### Short Stories

Unbroken (Free to Reader Group)

The Yellow Tandem

Milton

Stakeout

## ABOUT SAM SKYBORNE

Sam Skyborne is the proud author of a number of award winning novels and currently lives & loves in London (UK) while happily going on writing adventures across the globe ... or even further afield, as far as the mind will travel.

Connect with Sam:

Private Facebook Reader Group:
Facebook.com/groups/SamSkyborneGroup

Facebook Page: @SamSkybornePage

Instagram: @SamSkyborne

Sam's online home: SamSkyborne.com

Or drop Sam an email: mail@SamSkyborne.com

# FREE EBOOK!

Printed in Great Britain
by Amazon